I willed her to go on. I willed my letting go. Which philosopher claimed faith was a blind leap over a bottomless chasm? I leapt.

Did taking away all desire to stop her mean she'd won the ultimate victory? And was it a victory for both of us, or just for her? Was this merely a different kind of control than Anne exerted?

Rhonda said my name. At least she said "Silver," my name when I am a hot-blooded dyke stud, a name I had long ago cast off. Silver it was. I was glad she at least knew whom she was with. For intense seconds when I was careening off walls in my agony/ecstasy, I didn't know who she was, who I was, where I was.

"Silver," she wailed again.

"Rhonda," I echoed. An earthy, sexual name, sounds which pulled at my innards, pulled something out of my guts that I didn't know was there. Rhonda.

Never had I had sex like that. I wondered if it would ever be possible again. Who cared? To have it once in a lifetime might be enough.

CAROL
SCHMIDT

The Naiad Press, Inc.
1993

Printed in the United States of America on acid-free paper
First Edition

Edited by Christine Cassidy
Cover design by Pat Tong and Bonnie Liss
(Phoenix Graphics)
Typeset by Sandi Stancil

Library of Congress Cataloging-in-Publication Data

Schmidt, Carol, 1942—
Silverlake heat / by Carol Schmidt.
p. cm.
ISBN 1-56280-031-0 : $9.95
1. Lesbians—Fiction. I. Title.
PS3569.C51544S56 1993
813′.54—dc20 92-40089
CIP

This book is dedicated to Norma Hair, a most surprising woman chock full of devious plot twists, unconditional inspiration and other delicious inventions. My partner of fourteen years, she deserves but would not accept a joint byline.

About the Author

Carol Schmidt has been a newspaper reporter, publishing editor, public relations director for a medical research institute affiliated with UCLA, and co-owner with Norma Hair of Words & Numbers, a business services firm in the Silverlake region of Los Angeles. Now she and Norma live in a hundred-year-old church and school that they are turning into a home in rural Michigan, close to where they both grew up.

Her community involvement has included registering voters in the South in the '60s, organizing feminist consciousness-raising groups from 1968 through to the '80s, serving on the state board of California NOW, co-founding White Women Against Racism, and serving as co-chair of Sunset Junction Neighborhood Alliance, the organization which puts on the annual Sunset Junction Street Fair that brings together a quarter-million residents of Silverlake-Echo Park to celebrate their diversity.

Schmidt wrote reviews and a column ("Country Womyn/City Dyke") for the Los Angeles *Lesbian News* in the '80s and won three first place writing awards from the National Gay and Lesbian Press Association. She has also been published in hundreds of newspapers, small magazines and anthologies. Her second novel of suspense will be published by Naiad in 1994.

CHAPTER ONE

What finally threw me over the edge was the umpteenth letter from yet another organization I'd never heard of, thanking Anne and me profusely for our "Gold Circle" patronage and requesting our presence at the Sheraton Universal for yet another rubber-chicken banquet at which we would be the guests of honor.

I was living Anne's life. What had happened to my own?

For weeks I'd agonized over the how and when.

Even sometimes the why. But I kept coming up with the unmistakable truth that it was time.

Which is how I found myself standing in our bedroom doorway and looking down at Anne snoring softly in our waterbed. It was three a.m. — I'd just gotten home from the bar that Anne and I co-own — and I'd been arguing with myself *ad nauseam* until I finally decided. It was time.

The muggy April night had never cooled. Anne's salt-and-pepper ringlets clung to her damp pink cheeks. When she slept she always reminded me of my grandmother who lived out in the country in Michigan, one of the few good memories of my childhood. And when I thought of my grandmother I automatically thought of good cooking. Anne was just as good a cook as my grandmother, though instead of stuffed porkchops Anne specialized in Szechuan chicken.

So I was thinking of food. Anything to put off a miserable job.

Four lumps at the foot and another alongside her cheek took advantage of the king-size bed. Though I couldn't distinguish the animals in the dark I would bet that the three little dogs (Shih Tzu, Pomeranian and Pekinese), a Siamese cat, and any of the four alley cats she'd rescued were snoozing right along with her.

As if on command, the gold shaggy Shih Tzu gurgled and tossed in her sleep like the overgrown baby she was. We didn't have the aromas of perfumes or cosmetics in our home; our signature scent was flea dip.

Holding my place was Radar, my white German shepherd, the only one who was awake and alert.

Her big ears stood up and twitched, searching the air for identifiable sounds. As I watched, her ears lay back in guilt. Without my ordering, she shifted herself sideways and let her ninety-pound body slide out of bed. The "waveless mattress" adjusted, each animal riding a crest.

Radar padded sheepishly out of the room. It wasn't necessary this time. I wouldn't be lying down next to Anne. I doubted I'd ever sleep in that spot again.

How was I going to break up with this woman I'd lived with for nineteen, nearly twenty, years?

It could wait until tomorrow.

No, I'd been chicken about this for weeks, maybe months. Actually for a year or more. Now or never.

"Anne. *Anne.* Wake up, we have to talk."

She turned, causing ripples that dislodged five pets and made them emote in varied groans and snorts. Anne coughed, rolled back, and edged the navy paisley sheet over her one exposed pink-lobed ear as if to cut out all sounds. The Pomeranian raised his fox head, pointed a sharp, accusing snout at me and growled.

"Anne! Please wake up. I need to talk to you." Five pairs of brown, green and blue eyes were open now, but not Anne's.

I was being unreasonable; tomorrow would be soon enough. Anne needed her sleep. She'd just gone through a Saturday, her busiest day at the clinic. No, she could sleep late on Sunday. If she'd be able to get back to sleep after hearing me out.

Maybe it wouldn't bother her at all?

Who was I kidding?

My thoughts jumped back and forth between

rationalization and reason, and I could no longer tell the difference. The beginning of a headache throbbed in my left temple.

"Anne." My voice was too loud, even to me. This time she opened her eyes in panic, squinted at me, then closed them again, reassured by my relative calm that there wasn't a fire or burglary. Maybe I was being too cool. A therapeutic scream right now might be good for my emotional health, if not for Anne's, but I didn't want to scare her. What I was about to do was bad enough.

"What's wrong?" Anne peered out from under drooping eyelids, apparently decided I wasn't going to leave her alone, and reached for a yellow cotton shortie robe. She felt around on the nightstand for her slippers — you don't dare leave slippers on the floor because of the Pomeranian. These were oversized slippers in the shape of fuzzy schnauzers, so cute I wouldn't have even blamed the Pom.

Anne yawned and stretched along the headboard shelves for her glasses. The first thing you see when you look at Anne is her wide, pale eyes behind those royal blue frames. Her eyes are lighter now, but twenty years ago they were deep blue, contrasting with almost-black hair that had curled loosely to her shoulders. Now she wears what we used to call a poodle cut, and after that a white Afro. She calls it utilitarian hair.

When had the feelings melted? You'd have to say we were still friends, on the rare occasions when we saw each other off of a dais. But somehow over the past few years Anne and I had become barely more than roommates. And whose fault was that, I wondered, not for the first time. No one's, I'd already decided.

Had Anne's feelings really gone away? That was the question. I didn't have the answer, and I was afraid of the pain my talk was going to cause if she still thought of us as lovers. Funny, the obvious things, the important things, two people never talk about.

"We've got to talk, Anne."

She groaned what might have been a curse, wavering between the bed and me. "Good grief, Laney, can't it wait until morning?"

"It's important."

Anne opened her blue eyes wide behind her glasses. "All right, all right. So where do you want to talk?" Her eyes were wary now, darting, not meeting mine. After that first direct contact, she'd backed away instantly.

"Um, the kitchen."

She got out of the waterbed in her inimitable way, her rear end sunk to the bottom of the mattress while she shoved herself up and out. A little rounder than when we first got together, Anne's body is still attractive. I looked away; it was like catching a glimpse of a naked stranger in a department store dressing room.

Her pubic hair was salt and pepper now, too, and sparser than I'd remembered. Why don't they tell you in sex education classes, when they get around to talking about the maturing of the female body, that the curly short hair that grows in at puberty starts to fall out after menopause? Soon it would be my turn; my crotch itched at the thought.

Wriggling into her robe, carrying her slippers, she padded behind me to the kitchen. We sat down at the round oak table while she wrestled the schnauzers onto her feet. Anne got back up, poured herself a goblet of skim milk, and sat down again. She waited, rubbing her eyes, glancing at me between her fingers. "What's up? Are you in trouble?"

"Anne, we haven't made love in what, a year?"

She perked up and smoothed her hair.

"Oops, that was the wrong way to begin." My throat was closing, not letting the words come through. "Anne, our relationship has changed. We're not really lovers anymore. Friends, yes, and I never want that to change. But I've been feeling that we've grown apart. There's a lot I feel as if I'm missing out on, like I'm living in your house, in your life, not my own life. We've talked about this . . ."

Anne's face denied that she had ever understood what I had tried many times before to say.

"It's like . . . I'm Pygmalion to your Henry Higgins, and it's time for me to live my own life." She bristled at this analogy, as she had the first time I'd used it. "You don't want to hear this, you won't see how controlling you are, and how I've let myself be controlled. It's nobody's fault. It's just how we are together."

Her refusal to understand made me feel angry. I felt trapped, and not for the first time. I tried another tack: "It's not just that, I have to admit. I miss the passion, the excitement of a different kind of love . . ."

"You mean animal magnetism," she interjected

with a sarcastic, knowing grin, despite her sleepy eyes.

I blushed in the dark. Anne and I had had this fight several times when we'd first gotten together, when I had attempted to defend my flirting with other women. A few months of couples therapy had helped us to establish that I was "merely" afraid of commitment, that I'd kept from making a full commitment by keeping my interest in other women, that I was hanging onto a belief that I didn't deserve it. And then I'd committed.

I could see now that way back then I had also been trying to keep some of my independence, to keep from being swallowed up in the great generosity and loving that was pouring from Anne, swallowing up all that I had been, turning my life around from the drifting soul I was into half of a perfect couple. Anne's idea of a perfect couple.

My old flirtatiousness had been the last remnant of my independence. And now, at age forty-eight, going on forty-nine, soon to be fifty, that self had reemerged. I couldn't bear the thought of turning fifty and of celebrating our twentieth anniversary just the way we were — somehow those decade turning points lay heavily on me, as if once I let them pass without question I was doomed to stay in the same limbo for the rest of my life. Midlife crisis — a joke, but real. Maybe this time I could make it on my own — with the undisputed help of all that Anne had taught me, given me, shown me.

"Anne, you have done so much for me, it's beyond comprehension. When we met I was just drifting along from job to job, still getting over the shock of the Army giving me the shaft, going from lover to lover, drinking too much, not a penny to my name, and you turned my life around. I owe you so much."

Anne was rigid as I spoke. It was no use.

"Look, I've tried in one way or another to talk about this before — I need to know more about our money, about what's really mine. I need to make more decisions on my own. Our life is good, but it's like I'm in your pocket, and I put myself there because it's so warm and comfortable, but maybe it's time for the baby kangaroo to emerge."

She wouldn't meet my eyes. Her index finger drew circles on the table.

"You're not hearing me." I heaved a deep sigh. This was not easy. "Anne, I'm going to start seeing other women."

That did jolt her upright.

"There's someone else." Her voice was flat.

"No, not somebody else, but I see lots of women who are starting to look interesting." One redhead in particular had drawn my eye at the bar, but I had never said a word to her. The thought that now I might made me shiver.

Anne's finger trembled as it inscribed smaller and smaller circles against the wood grain. My words sounded cold, even to me. I went back to what seemed safer.

"I want you to have our — your — money people draw up some sort of separate financial arrangements. I've been thinking about this, and I don't know how I could afford to buy you out on the bar, and I know you don't want to sell the house. I have no idea how to handle this financially. We're all so tangled up that I don't know if anyone can figure out what's fair, but I want us to try. Maybe I should move into the office at the bar, the way Ray used to do when he owned it, but then I couldn't keep Radar."

I shuddered at the thought of living in that tiny single room, one thin wall away from the bar noise. "I'm going to move into Rob's room for the time being — he won't be back from school for a few months, if he comes back for the summer at all." Rob is Anne's son, in premed at Stanford. "So maybe it'll work out for us to be roommates . . ."

She still hadn't said a word. *Controlling bitch.* No, I didn't think that. This was a woman I'd loved for nearly twenty years. Who still loved me.

"Anne, I'm so sorry . . ."

In desperation I glanced around the kitchen, trying to find a way out of this conversation, a conversation I never thought I would have to have. From the top of the spice rack, a Portuguese ceramic rooster mocked me with his heavily lashed orange eye. Chicken, the cock taunted. I took a deep breath and said it once more.

"Anne, it's over. I want us to separate our money. I've tried —"

I stopped, feeling helpless. I was talking about money, not the pain I was causing Anne. My mind had been on the financial problems of the split more than on the human being I once loved, actually would always love, but could no longer live with. We were going to have to peel away this relationship like an onion, but with real tears.

Her face was a mausoleum of deadened life held in marble. For a second I wanted to wipe it all away and tell her I didn't mean it. I waited.

Anne's breaths were shallow and rapid. Rubbing her eyes and running her pale fingers through her curls, she stared out the window into the dark. Our kitchen was not the only oasis of light in the three a.m. blackness. A few blocks away a police helicopter shone a beam down into backyards. Faraway sirens wailed.

Finally, Anne was crying. Just one tear so far, but there would be more, in the privacy of her room. *Her* room now.

"You're really serious about this," she said. She put the rest of her milk back in the fridge. "You said you'll sleep in Rob's room? That's fine. We'll have to talk about this some more. Not now. I'm going back to bed."

But not to sleep, I was sure. She walked off, holding herself rigid compared to the shuffling sleepy self who had walked into the kitchen moments before.

At least there hadn't been a loud, angry scene. Not yet anyway.

Watching her, I felt again that I was making a huge mistake. I couldn't hurt this woman who had been so good to me for all those years. Who had saved my life.

"I loved you, I really did," I cried out.

She hesitated, just a second, frozen in space like a rabbit sighting a hawk plummeting down on her. She walked on.

The door to Anne's room, her room, closed gently. Scuffling sounds told me the dogs and cats were settling back in position after Anne's brief absence, resenting me for having taken her away, forgiving me now that I had let her get back to them. There would be a lot of grouchy pets underfoot in the morning. I didn't even want to think about what Anne's condition would be.

With her gone, I had to sit with the consequences of my decision. The kitchen was small, an island of bright light almost blinding in contrast to the claustrophobic darkness, the ceramic chicken still mocking me with its cold eye, and I was alone.

Not totally. Radar plodded in on her clumsy big feet and plopped herself down so that her head fell against my hand. I scratched the white Shepherd absentmindedly. She moaned in contentment.

For a second I thought of a film clip I'd seen once, of a Moslem man divorcing his wife by simply saying to her three times, "I divorce you."

It shouldn't be so easy to break up a twenty-year relationship. For once I felt deprived of the laws that protect relationships legitimized by marriage. Ordinarily I didn't want the government in my private life, but somehow I figured I'd be feeling better if some court official had said I was legally divorced, had given it some finality.

Not that divorce proceedings would have been pleasant — my father did it four times, and I didn't like watching the women he dumped scramble to pick up the pieces. His drinking made the breakups messier.

Now what do I do?

Suddenly I felt very stupid and alone. But at least I was being honest. No way could I ever sleep with Anne again, feeling the way I did. I'd learned

— earned — a smidgeon of self-respect during the past nineteen years. Anne had helped me, and now look what it had gotten her.

I shook off the feeling and padded into Rob's bedroom and put clean sheets on the day bed. The twin mattress seemed strange and lumpy after a king-size waterbed. A shared waterbed.

Radar snuggled against the side of the bed and let her head fall across my chest. Doggie breath and all, her company was needed. I tried to sleep.

CHAPTER TWO

Anne and I managed to not see each other for more than a week — I stayed in my new room until she left for the clinic each morning, she went to bed before I got home from the bar each night. My emotional state zigzagged between skydiving and entombment. I was free — except for some guilt, though I couldn't see what I should feel guilty about. I was trying to do the right thing, as best I knew it.

And meanwhile the woman had returned to the bar. The woman whose first quick, wordless glance at me across the room had hinted at possibilities.

She had left almost immediately, that first visit, and the second was not much longer. I'd picked up a definite feeling that she was a scared babydyke. And that she was interested in me.

Had I lied to Anne? Was this phantom woman the real reason I'd broken up with Anne? No, I could honestly say, after much self-analysis. I was just sick of being the tall dyke in the silver-trimmed tuxedo on Anne's arm. Maybe the redhead's appearance had speeded things up? I didn't think so — I remembered my anger at the gilt-edged invitation, at all the gilt-edged invitations.

Friday night was my usual AIDS Aid benefit; Larry and Dave set up their literature table in the redhead's corner. She'd sat there twice and in my mind it was her corner. In fact, it was the AIDS Aid canister left on the counter for donations all week which made me first notice her. Just before she'd left, she'd put in a carefully folded hundred-dollar bill, and Carmen, my main bartender, had come running to tell me about it as the redhead exited.

I'd dropped everything to catch a closer glimpse of this benefactor who had been almost inconspicuous till then. As inconspicuous as a truly drop-dead gorgeous woman can be. As inconspicuous as any attractive woman could be to a dyke who hadn't had sex in a year and who was thinking about seeing other women. She'd driven off in a light yellow Mercedes convertible — not safe for a high-crime area like Silverlake. She must live in some remote suburb.

"Do you have to sit there?" I asked Larry and Dave, aware of the crankiness in my voice. Why should I feel possessive of an empty space?

They looked startled, then started to move the table. "Oh, it's okay, I don't know why I said that," I apologized. They still offered to find a different spot for their display, but I insisted.

She only came on Saturdays anyway. Or did I dare presume a pattern on the basis of two nights?

This time I really read the *Safer Sex for Lesbians* booklet. Things were a little different from the days when I used to play around. I thought of the woman's innocent round face, her shyness, her open green-blue eyes. I couldn't imagine her using needles, or sleeping with men at risk, or engaging in bloodletting S & M sexual practices.

"Hey, Silly, how ya been?"

Who still called me that?

A strong hand grabbed my shoulder affectionately and wheeled me around to face an old friend, Maxine Carruthers. Anne despised her, probably because Max was one of my old butch drinking buddies. She still wore our then-standard black leather jacket, men's pants and shirt, though she'd left off the tie. I'd gone through a clothes metamorphosis through the years with Anne and her feminist political correctness. Max's leather jacket sure looked good. Now that I was alone, maybe I'd pick up another one. It was too hot out for that jacket, but it sure made a statement.

My face got red just thinking of the home movies Anne took of me one night with Max at the bar. The films had sent me right to AA. I haven't had a drink in nineteen years, either. That was one of the things for which I owed Anne beyond the possibility of repayment. *And look what I've done to her.* I had to get rid of that thought right away.

"Hey, Max, you look terrific," I lied. "Long time no see. What brings you out tonight — didn't you move south? Laguna Beach somewhere?"

"Yeah, well, I'm back. Couldn't take all those gorgeous young rich bodies. Had to come back to the down-home folks."

Despite the great jacket, Max didn't look any too good. She'd always worn a deep tan, and the years of sun had caught up to her, making her face look like bark. She'd tried to cover up her own gray hair with one of those tony ash-blonde dye jobs, but roots showed through the streaks.

"Gimme a light beer, dammit," Max ordered with a voice gone deep from years of smoking. I'd quit that, too, when Anne had made me go out on the porch to smoke all the time. It got to feeling pretty stupid when the rainy season came, standing outside my own house smoking wet Camels. How many years more of my life did I owe Anne?

"A toast," Max said, when I brought her beer myself, waving away my other bartenders. Carmen and Nancy pretty much took care of the entire bar for me; I just hung around to keep my hand in, giving special service to old friends. I lifted my Diet Pepsi can.

"You still off the sauce?" Max looked puzzled. She never did like the new me. I nodded.

"A toast to love," she said, too loudly. Heads turned her direction as she chug-a-lugged.

I sipped, then asked, "You're in love?"

"With love," she laughed. "Still looking. Hey, what you reading?" She picked up *Safer Sex for Lesbians.* "Ain't this some scary shit? At least dykes don't have to worry."

"Not exactly," I said. "You'd better read the book."

She did, dropping ashes on the counter as she read. I mopped them up with a damp rag and left the counter wet. She didn't notice.

"Look at this, this book says to use a rubber dam for going down!" Max pointed to the paragraph. "That'd be as romantic as licking a tennis shoe. Maybe I should just forget about love, hey?"

"Things have sure changed," I agreed. But the changes hadn't affected my personal life until now.

I had to get away for a minute. I left Max's end of the bar and retreated to my office in back. The previous owner had lived in the office, which was equipped with a sofabed, shower, desk, and a wall unit that incorporated a small fridge, sink, and two gas burners. Sure, it's against the law to live in a business establishment, but lots of people do it.

I used to use the sofabed some nights when I didn't feel like driving home after the bar closed. Ray had had good taste; the sofabed was real leather, a rich maroon that would have fit in at a downtown law office. The leather felt cool against my neck, calming me down. Anne always had me do deep-breathing and stretching exercises when I was uptight; ironic I should be using her advice now.

When I felt better I decided I could face Max — and the world — again.

"What's the matter, Laney? Are you feeling all right?" Larry asked as I passed by his table. "Hey, I could take over the bar if you want to go home. Carmen and Nancy have things under control. We'll probably have a small crowd tonight."

"Why?" I asked.

"All the regulars are probably at the Bowl for the Sweet Honey in the Rock concert." He looked at me quizzically and went back to talking with Dave.

I'd forgotten all about the Hollywood Bowl concert, a benefit for women political candidates. It was exactly the kind of event Anne and I would have attended, up front in a patrons' box for $150 each. For Sweet Honey in the Rock, I would have actually enjoyed it.

Had she mentioned something about it? Did we have tickets? We must have bought them long ago. Anne kept track of things like that for me. I wondered idly if she'd gone anyway. Alone. Or with somebody else.

"Why so glum, chum?" Max asked, smiling at her own rhyme. Tonight everything annoyed me.

I told her I'd broken up with Anne.

"Hey, no shit. You crazy? Why'd you do a dumb thing like that?" Even though Max had always sensed Anne's feelings against her, Max was one of Anne's admirers.

I wasn't at all sure why, especially as I scanned the small crowd and looked for the woman who might never be there.

I tried to tell Max about how boxed in I'd felt lately, and how maybe it was my time to finally grow up.

Max shook her head, then her face lit up. "I get it, there's somebody else."

"No, there isn't," I argued. Max guffawed. "I mean, there isn't anybody I've even talked to." I sighed and decided to say it all, even though it would make me look like a fool. A preadolescent voice from the '50s still lodged in my head taunted, "Silly Samms, Silly Samms" — that was my nickname in grade school when I didn't fit in and the rest of the kids didn't know what to make of me, any more than I did.

Max wasn't exactly a nominee for Psychologist of the Year, but there was nobody else I'd been able to talk to about the breakup. I definitely needed to dump. And I wanted some input on my fantasy woman.

"There's this redhead who's come into the bar twice, and she just sits in the corner and watches. She looks scared, I think she's a straight woman wondering about coming out, and I want to approach her, but it wouldn't be a light kind of thing like it usually is with a babydyke, where you know she's just playing around for a while and just wants to have her first lesbian sex experience and then you can't tell what she'll do but it won't be a longtime thing —"

I wondered if I was even coherent, the way my words tumbled out. I took another deep breath and slowed down. "I know, I know, I did that a few times in the old days, but this isn't like that." I hastened to cover up those memories. "I get the feeling this could be different."

"You haven't even talked to her?" Max asked.

I felt ridiculous. "Except for asking what she wanted to drink, right."

"And you think she's straight?"

"Right. She's wearing a ring."

"And married, too?"

I could only nod.

"And she's just come into the bar twice, and you don't know if she'll ever be back?" Max's voice was incredulous.

I lowered my eyes. It certainly did sound stupid. I gave Max another beer. She shook her head and downed half of it in one gulp. I took a seat next to her.

"Who was your first crush?" I asked her, to change the subject, but not really.

"Doris Day." Max's eyes lit up at the memory. "I wanted to be Rock Hudson in *Pillow Talk.*"

"You came close. Mine was on the movie screen too, only it was an ad for a flower shop that ran between the features every Saturday night when my folks took me to the Westown. That was in Detroit — did they have ads at the movies in L.A. back then?"

"I was in Des Moines." Max wrinkled her forehead. "I don't think we did. Can't recall. Was your real mother still around then?"

"No, dad's wife number two. Maybe three. Anyway, in the ad there was this redhead with this incredibly shiny, new-penny-bright wavy long hair, down to her shoulders. She wore a bright turquoise strapless evening gown, with a full skirt not quite to the floor, and her high heels matched the dress. She waltzed through the flower shop like a ballerina, picking up a rose here, a carnation there, making a bouquet."

I sighed, remembering the ad as clearly as if I were still nine years old. "Every time the commercial came on I'd tell my stepmother that I wanted to marry that girl when I grew up. She used to laugh and tell me that I meant I wanted to *look* like the girl when I grew up, but I knew what I meant."

I chuckled aloud. "Maybe she suspected too. Right after the ad started to run, my stepmother bought me a Halloween outfit that was supposed to be Cinderella in a light aqua dress — it even had a rhinestone tiara and glass, rather plastic, slippers. She got mad when I wouldn't wear it. When she tried to put it on me anyway I ripped it to shreds and went trick-or-treating as Roy Rogers instead. She told my dad when he got home and he slapped me around and threw out my candy."

Max smiled wryly along with me at the scene. "Bet it wasn't funny at the time."

"I can still see that redhead twirling around on her heels in that turquoise ballgown. I dreamed of taking her to the prom."

"Did you ever go to your prom?" Max asked.

"Oh, yeah, sure. I sat home and reread the Army recruiting brochure, getting up the courage to enlist. Did you?"

"Me neither." Max lit still another cigarette. "So you're saying this redhead who came into the bar gives you the hots like your first crush."

"Something like that. She walks the same way, like a dancer. She's built like a dancer too, sort of like Paula Abdul, compact and strong. And then there's that gorgeous hair. You're right, it doesn't make a lot of sense. But if Doris Day walked through that door, wouldn't you take a chance on her?"

"Suppose so. 'Scuse me." Max swaggered to the restroom, ogling the other customers on the way.

I pictured the mysterious woman as she had looked the last time, sitting at the end of the bar in the corner, her tanned hands coddling a glass of white wine. She looked at her glass when anyone glanced her way. Her red-gold hair, pushed back from her face by a paisley scarf worn as a headband, fell forward in shiny waves to her shoulders, shadowing her face. When I caught a glimpse of her face it looked perfectly round, and her round blue-green eyes looked startled when they met mine. Then vaguely amused. Then she dropped her gaze back to her glass. *Shy* wasn't quite the word. And then I'd seen the ring. And decided she was a babydyke.

She wore makeup. Peach lips. A definite attempt to make her face look less round with peach blush. Those big eyes framed with thick brown mascara and liner, artfully applied. None of Anne's femme friends ever wore the stuff — maybe not because of political correctness but because they never could achieve quite the look she'd accomplished. Except the young "lipstick lesbians" who seemed to belong to a whole new generation. Something about this woman made me sure she wasn't in that category.

Sure, I knew all the feminist arguments — Anne is a devout feminist — against the artificial, costly, dangerous goop women are supposed to put on to be "acceptable" to men and to fuel the cosmetics industry. There had been no men there tonight except for one bartender, who wouldn't care what kind of makeup *any* woman had on. All the feminist arguments almost made me feel guilty for admiring the way the redhead looked in makeup. Still, there was natural beauty underneath, it was easy to see.

I preferred to stay away from women who were just discovering they were lesbians, ever since a couple of nasty experiences when I was younger. Much younger.

One "straight" woman had sat bolt upright in bed after a delicious night of abandoned lovemaking, announced I was a pervert for seducing her to my "terrible" life (even though she'd come on to me first), and split in a flushed fury. A car crash on her way home left her with a bashed-in face that took plastic surgery to bring back almost to normal. Of course it hadn't been my fault. Tell my gut that.

Yet another straight woman, when lesbian life wasn't all she'd hoped for, had blamed me for "corrupting" her, even mentioned a lawsuit. And another . . . in nine years of active lesbian life before I'd settled in with Anne I'd slept with a lot of women, searching for that special person. Anne had been the one.

Too many memories crowded my mind, helping me to avoid where I was right now. There'd been too many women. Too many sloshed nights and woozy mornings and empty afternoons. Anne had changed all that. And it had been good. Very good. Only somewhere along the last nineteen — nearly twenty — years, our pleasant life had spoiled like Gallo Hearty Burgundy turned to vinegar.

Too many women were out there just like I'd been, just like I was again. An involuntary shudder jiggled me in my seat.

This woman was different, I'd felt it. I tried not to remember all my previous one a.m. desperate searches for anyone who might do, trying to read something into a vacuous face. This woman looked real. I felt a wanting low in my belly, so strong I was almost nauseous.

"You're thinking about her now, aren't you?" Max was back. Something in her voice made me think she might even be jealous.

I nodded, almost ashamed. But I shouldn't have been — I'd broken up with Anne before allowing myself to even think about another woman. So what if it was a little quick. I didn't choose the timing. I had to grab onto her because she could be special and I didn't want to chance missing her because I had to wait some imaginary "proper" time.

The memory of the redhead was as overpowering as the feelings I'd had when I'd seen her last. She'd worn a leaf-green sleeveless patterned sweater and slim camel skirt that ended just above her knees. She'd crossed her long legs as she perched on a barstool, one snakeskin-sandaled high heel dangling slightly from her manicured toes. No one else in Samms' looked anything like her, not even since the renaissance in dressing up.

A solid rounded puffy gold heart like a teenager would wear hung from a thin chain around her neck. The diamond on her left hand could have paid off a mortgage.

And I was the only one she'd really looked at in the half hour she'd sat on that stool, sipping the one wine, finally slipping away without a word, an exact repeat of the visit she'd made the previous Saturday night. Without the hundred-dollar drop. I wondered now if she'd used the donation to get my attention. *Don't flatter yourself, Laney.*

The second time I'd gotten a hint of a smile. Directed at me alone.

Why was she slumming in a Silverlake lesbian bar? Was she the stereotypical latent wife who finally wanted out of her hypocritical life, no matter what the cost? It was going to cost her, probably more than she knew. But there could be a hefty payoff, like maybe finally being free.

How rhapsodical I made it all sound. I was fantasizing, romanticizing. I had no idea about who or what she really was.

It would be dangerous to get involved with a woman like that. Let her come out with a neighbor while their husbands were at work. No, for some reason she'd chosen to come to Samms', and to smile at me.

"Shit," Max said after I'd finished rambling on about the breakup. "You're dumber than I thought. That's how you see Anne? Somehow I never figured you for a kept woman. Shouldn't you have waited until you had something going before you gave up a sure thing?"

I couldn't defend myself against this perfect logic. Still, I'd had to do it. "It was the right thing to do," I said, feeling helpless.

"Yeah, sure, if you say so." Max finished her beer and ordered another. I took my time getting it and brought a dish of pretzels to diffuse the alcohol. I had no tolerance for drunks anymore. I was quick to use the old "86." Maybe that's why I had such a nice, stable, quiet, older clientele, even though the newer bars had flash and youth. Plenty of makeup and skirts at the new hotspots.

"Hey, didn't I just read about you and Anne as lesbian pioneers or some such shit? And here you go and split up. It was in one of those bar rags."

Maxine was making me more and more angry, but she continued, oblivious. "Yeah, I remember now. It was the *Lesbian News,* and it sounded like you both could walk on water."

She gulped her drink. "But now that you mention it, I remember getting something else from the article. Yeah, I remember saying to myself, 'There's trouble in paradise between you two.' Holy shit, so it really happened."

I hadn't read that into the article myself. It had been embarrassing to read my life story out there for the whole world to see.

How soon would all the organizations drop me? How about the AIDS Aid board — that was the one group I really worked for because it arranged person-to-person caregiving and stayed out of the politics. Anne and I were like a divorcing straight couple, but instead of dividing kids we'd have to divide organizations.

Oh well, these things would work themselves out, I assured myself. I didn't care about the recognition, I'd keep holding benefits at Samms' and making my own donations when I could. When I knew how much I actually had to live on. Why hadn't I paid more attention when Anne tried to teach me about money? It hadn't been totally her fault I was so ignorant, I realized regretfully. It had been a relief to no longer have to scrounge for money, to turn all those worries over to her. So maybe I was being extra hard on her. I had to, to keep up my resolve.

I wouldn't miss attending board meetings. I always made the same tired jokes about "bored" meetings whenever we attended one, and Anne always answered, "Look under the board and find your anger." Anne was hot on psychology. I downed my Diet Pepsi.

"Look at that chick — vice squad written all over her," Max said. "Cops been bothering you much lately?"

"Not me, mainly the men's bars." I wanted to add, "Don't call women 'chicks,' " but it was useless with Max. I'd only told her a thousand times.

Max watched the probable cop meander through the bar, looking at the younger faces, checking for the sign on the wall giving the Fire Department's maximum allowed capacity, attempting to inconspicuously count heads. Many of the heads she was counting glared at her.

"Remember how it used to be in the old days, when all our bars had some sort of bird name so we could tell?" Max said as I wiped spots off glasses. "Remember the Blue Parrot and the White Peacock? Remember going to the old Rockin' Robin in the Valley? I really thought the two of us were going to hit it off that night, 'cept you couldn't stop being butch long enough."

"Neither could you." I grinned in spite of myself. Max liked to recall the good old days. They weren't that great, as I remembered them now. What I could remember. But I could get into a little trip down memory lane to keep my mind off the redhead who wasn't there.

"Hey, what about the Pink Parakeet?" Max's eyes glistened.

"Now you're talking the old, old days," I said. "Umm, remember how Jack always made sure there was an equal number of men and women, and when he thought there was trouble he'd flash the lights and we'd all switch partners — instant straight bar?"

Maxine roared. "Yeah, and remember how he used red napkins for any customer he thought might be vice squad?" I chuckled too. And then I looked over at the AIDS Aid table and grew silent. Jack was gone.

Max kept trying to get me back into the mood. "You do something different with the patio 'round back? All those twinkling lights in the trees, I thought you'd had an invasion of fireflies."

It was an idea borrowed from the short-lived Flamingo on Sunset around the corner from my Hyperion site in Silverlake. Samms' used to be Silly Samms', before I grew up some and let myself drop my childhood nickname. It was a men's bar in the "good old days," so the entrance is hidden.

I keep Samms' running in the black with all the marketing gimmicks — Samms' T-shirt giveaways to keep my name out there, a baseball team, talent shows, potlucks, Toys for Tots collections. I even put out a newsletter on a laptop computer, full of newsy gossip. I was proud of the place.

As if reading my mind, Max asked, "What you gonna do about the bar?"

I choked on my second soft drink. "We haven't talked about it yet."

She shook her head. "The whole thing sounds crazy to me. Hey, look, that woman coming in the door. Sounds like the chick you described. That her?"

The fact that Max would dare call *my* woman a "chick" especially infuriated me. As if she *were* my woman. My head was spinning. I almost didn't want to look around.

It was her.

"Max, get lost," I ordered, my eyes glued on the redhead. Her round face and bright eyes looked confused; her place was taken. I wished I had ordered Larry and Dave to find another spot.

"Hey, aren't you gonna introduce me? She *is* a looker." Max's voice was throaty. I wanted to wallop her.

"I tell you, get lost."

"When you gonna make your move?"

"I said, get out of here." My anger seethed.

"You afraid I'll embarrass you in front of her? Make a move myself?"

"Get out!" I whispered, but my intent was unmistakable.

"Hey, you're serious. I don't see what she sees in an old geezer like you. Okay, okay, see when I come back next," Max said as she drank the last of her beer and picked up her wallet. "I know when I'm not wanted." She whistled the melody to "I Got Friends in Low Places," looking back over her shoulder at me as she left, slowly, very slowly.

Just to further annoy me as she exited, Max dared to touch the newcomer on the shoulder. The woman recoiled.

"Sweet thing," Max said, winking back at me.

The redhead looked frightened, her round eyes growing even larger. I smiled at her and nodded toward the seat Max had just vacated. I tried to project a cool, non-threatening image.

The moment Max went out the door, my anger disappeared, replaced by old-fashioned anxiety. My breath caught in my throat, choking away the words I'd rehearsed.

The woman came over and sat down in front of me.

CHAPTER THREE

Without asking I poured her white wine.

She didn't say anything, so I said it for her: "I remembered."

Startled, she looked up at me with those round green-blue eyes. It was too much too soon, I worried, though it was mild as an opener compared to what I hear all the time at the bar. I hadn't "dated" in nineteen years, so all lines sounded strange on my lips.

"I'm sorry, I didn't mean to be so bold." Ouch, that sounded stilted too.

"I'm flattered," she said.

Good. Now what should I say? "I'm Laney Samms — welcome to my bar."

"I looked at your sign outside — it looks like it used to be called *Silly* Samms'." The question hung unspoken.

Damn my stinginess at not repainting immediately when the teal and coral paint job started to fade again. So should I do a song and dance, evade the question altogether, or be upfront from the start about who I am? I wavered, then decided on the truth. Tell her what it's like to be a dyke, what it used to be like. But in a light way, so she didn't get scared or overwhelmed.

"My parents named me Priscilla Elaine Samms, and they wanted a sweet little Priscilla Elaine in dotted swiss dresses and patent leather shoes. Instead they got a tomboy who grew into a six-foot lesbian."

Good again, she didn't flinch at the "L" word. Her green eyes swept up and down my body. It felt like instant sunburn. I kept talking, ignoring my flushed feelings.

"In the seventh grade I walked around all stoop-shouldered, trying to hide my height — and my feelings — and somebody nicknamed me Priscilly, then just Silly. It stuck. Took a while to outgrow it. When I did, I renamed the bar. Guess the paint's faded again."

She listened attentively, not scanning the rest of the patrons out of the corners of her eyes, the way most bar conversations seem to go. "I heard someone call you Silver the other night too."

"I get called a lot of things." I felt like the

adolescent girl who'd tried on names to find one that might make her insecurity go away.

"Why do they call you Silver? Your hair?"

I nodded. Watching her take in my thick white waves, I was embarrassed. Also glad I'd spent the money on a good haircut at P.J.'s after her second appearance.

"It's very attractive. Premature, Silver?"

I grimaced. The name sounded so obvious, coming from her. And my forty-eight years felt ancient as I sat next to her; she was in her late twenties, I guessed.

"I prefer Laney now. Or sometimes people call me Priscilla, or Sil, or anything else they come up with. Silver sounds so phony, and Silly is, well . . ." Again I felt like the gangly teenager.

"Why not Sam?"

I grimaced. "Sam Samms? Double male whammy. But some people call me that too. I hate it."

"It must give you an identity crisis — Priscilla, Elaine, Laney, Silly, Silver, Sil, Sam . . ." It was a sweet smile, even if there was a hint of mocking at the edges of those full peach lips. I felt myself tremble. Inconspicuously I clutched the edge of the counter.

"Maybe that's been my trouble all these years," I said, trying to make light of it. Maybe it *had* been my trouble, running from all those names. One of the troubles, anyway.

"Whatcha gonna be when you grow up, Silly? A Harlem Globetrotter clown?" A voice from my seventh grade taunted me in the back reaches of my consciousness. No, I was going to make my career in the Army. Maybe I'd make it all the way to general!

At least serve my twenty years and have a great pension for the rest of my life. Never would I have dreamed then that I'd be just a bar owner.

In my mind I heard Anne's voice rebuking me for putting myself down, reminding me of how far I'd come, of all the community service. For groups of her choice. I'd even been invited to serve on the Governor's Commission on Alcoholism, representing gay men and lesbians as well as bar owners, back when California had a Democratic governor who cared about such things.

My mind rebuffed the attempts to bolster my self-esteem. I was a nobody, unfit to be making overtures to this beautiful woman.

Still, it wouldn't stop me from trying.

I have these arguments with myself all the time. Right now I was a battlefield inside. The Army general who never was had settled for internal wars instead.

I watched her sip her drink until the thought hit me that I was being too obvious, maybe too threatening. I turned away to straighten glasses and missed the sight of her almost instantly. I glanced back, trying to hide my nervousness. My stomach ached.

"How'd you come to open a bar?" she asked. I wondered if she was really interested or just making conversation.

"Oh, I was grooming some dogs at minimum wage for a veterinarian who told me I could be doing more in my life. The next thing I knew we were going together and we opened this bar — nineteen years ago."

"Why a bar?" she asked. "If he thought you

should be doing more with your life, why not law school? Or teaching?"

"She," I said.

She bit her lip. "Of course. It would be a she. I'm new to this."

"I know."

"It shows?" She looked amused, not quite embarrassed.

I nodded. "To get back to what you just said — you don't think running a bar is doing much with my life?" How did she know that the same thought had been running through my mind?

"I guess I did say that, didn't I?" This time she actually blushed, a warm peach glow flowing up her cheeks. Maybe she didn't have on rouge. "I'm sorry."

"Don't be. It makes a lot of money, and I get to give it away to a lot of good causes."

"Like AIDS," she glanced toward the table in "her" old corner. Slipping off her stool, she went over to Larry and Dave and took some of the brochures. Dave looked over at me and scratched his short Afro in an overly deliberate way, like doing charades. His partner elbowed him in the ribs. So they'd been watching me. By morning Anne would know. The woman brought the brochures back with her, avoiding the inquisition that Dave had been about to launch.

"I noticed you put a hundred dollars in the canister the first night you were here."

"Is something wrong with that?"

"No, it was just . . . unusually generous."

"I can afford it." She put the pamphlets in her purse.

It was a denim satchel. For the first time I saw

that she wore sleek new jeans so blue that it must have been their first wearing, and a crisp red plaid cotton shirt unbuttoned one button lower than I would have. A lacy peach-colored bra silhouetted rounded cleavage.

"You came casual tonight."

"You noticed." She followed my eyes and one hand closed the daring white button.

"Definitely. Are you embarrassed?" She looked it.

"No, not really." She glanced around, then deliberately changed the subject. "Are you and this vet still together?"

"No," I said, quite honestly, immensely relieved. The past weeks of agony had been worth it to be able to say that one word of truth.

"So what else have you done in your life?"

"You're asking all the questions tonight." She wore a rose-scented perfume I'd never breathed before. I leaned closer.

"You'll have your turn," she said. "With questions. So what else do you do, Laney?"

"Time out to ask just one question — what's your name?"

"Rhonda."

"Rhonda what?"

She looked unsure, glancing around the rest of the bar quickly. Making a big decision, she said, "Rasmussen."

"Rhonda Rasmussen. And Laney Samms. Sounds good together." Immediately I regretted saying it.

"So we're together now?" she teased. Did she sense the same feeling of inevitability I did? Or was I really off the deep end this time?

"We're a pair for this instant, aren't we?" I

wanted her to at least acknowledge that, make it the start of a habit.

"I suppose so. That was your one question, out of turn. So tell me more about yourself."

"Let's see, you know about my childhood."

"I do?" Her smile twinkled. I basked in it.

"You got the highlights. A kid who never fit in. Oh, and my father was a drunk and my mom disappeared and I got shifted around through the years to his relatives and four wives. Typical happy childhood." I gave her the overview in a light tone of voice, smiling. That's the usual way I talk about those lost years.

She looked stricken. I wanted to kiss her for the way she showed her sympathy, not overdoing it, not shocked or scandalized, just . . . there.

I took a breath and went on. "So anyway, I joined the Army right after high school, thought I'd see the world and instead got stuck in the PR typing pool. The chairs were always the wrong height. Let's see, then I came out with my staff sergeant . . ."

" 'Came out' . . . you mean, admitted you were gay?"

" 'Admitted' isn't exactly the right word, it makes the process sound a bit dirty. I allowed myself to discover I was a lesbian, how about that?"

"Okay, I'm new at this. I may use the wrong terms."

"I know."

"Oh, right, you guessed already that I'm . . . coming out."

"Uh huh." I had to fight the need to reach out and touch that new-penny-bright hair. I had the feeling she wouldn't mind. Or was I deluding myself? Babydykes could go crazy in a split second if you forced their hand one second earlier than they were ready. Better to let her make all the moves.

"So tell me more."

"About what?" I had no idea what we'd been talking about. I was lost in her rose perfume, her soft peach lips, her bouncy red curls, the button she'd somehow undone again.

"You'd been telling me about the Army."

"Oh, yeah. Well, besides coming out, I learned one thing more."

"What's that?"

"I never want to be in another typing pool."

She laughed again, as if I'd been so clever and original, then asked, "So it's true what they say about women in the military?"

"What's that, we're all dykes?" Even from her, I didn't like the stereotype.

"I'm sorry. I can tell from your face that I was wrong. But you were in the Army, and you came out with your sergeant — it must have been accepted?"

"Yeah, sure, you never heard of the lavender purges." The straight world never does. "I got the ax a few months before my discharge — which made it dishonorable. I could only get make-do jobs — assembly line work, used-car sales, dog grooming, that kind of thing — until the ACLU got it reversed a few years ago. As for your original statement, sure, there are a lot of dykes in uniform. We're everywhere." I gave her a smile to show I didn't hold it against her. "You've got a lot to learn."

"About what?" There was a hint of defensiveness

in her voice. Even perched on her barstool, she'd backed up.

"About the life. That's what old-timers call it."

"Old-timers?"

"Lifelong lesbians. LLLs. It's a term from one of the heavy thinkers in the lesbian community. Then there's babydykes." I watched her face.

"Which are?" She wouldn't cop to anything yet.

"Which are women who one day realize they might be attracted to other women, and they start checking it out."

"By coming into a gay bar and watching." She looked embarrassed again.

"Uh huh. Are you?"

"Am I what?"

"A babydyke?" She backed up farther; I'd gone too fast. "Maybe you're just at the thinking-about-it stage. It's a big thing to face."

"How did *you* know?" She leaned forward again.

"That I'm a lesbian? How did you know that you were straight?" Her face was confused. I laughed. "That's a pretty standard lesbian answer to your question. You're supposed to be confused. The process is just as gradual and natural with gays and lesbians. And some never figure it out — only the lucky ones do." I grinned at her.

She smiled back. Such a smile. How could I stand upright to a smile like that?

"I always knew I was different," I continued. "I wasn't a Priscilla Elaine. I was a tomboy who got angry when other girls didn't want to climb trees and play cowboys anymore, especially at ten or eleven when they turned to boys. I didn't. Never could see anything in a man to attract me. Though I like men individually — some men." I looked at Larry and David, who were answering questions as one of my customers wrote out a check. "Those two are great."

"Only gay men?" Rhonda asked, turning back from the fundraising corner to tilt her head at me.

"Mostly, though that's all I deal with now. I've known a few decent straight men in my life. None that ever turned me on." I deliberately looked at her wedding ring.

She followed my glance and put her hands under the counter. "It's okay that you're married," I said softly. "Lots of babydykes start out married. A few even stay married, though that's a hard life, keeping two separate identities. Does your husband have any idea?"

"That I might be a . . . lesbian?"

I laughed aloud at her hesitancy. She was so cute. "It's a hard word to say, especially the first time."

"Is this funny to you? You see this all the time and it's old hat?" Her blue-green eyes glared.

I sobered up immediately. "I'm sorry. I'm not making fun of you. No, it's not old hat, though most coming-out lesbians go through certain stages, and I see the similarities." I reached out a hand for her shoulder, to steady her. She may have been trembling. It may have been me.

I took my hand back. "I don't want you to think I know everything that's going on inside you before you do. I don't. I want to know more about what you're thinking. It can't be easy. I might even be able to help you."

"How?" She glanced at me, then looked at her wine. She became very intent on sipping that wine. Yes, there was pain behind her eyes. It had started.

"Any way you want."

Now she dared to look right at me. She wanted answers. And I got the distinct feeling she wanted me.

Tentatively I put my hand on her shoulder once more. She let it stay there for a full three seconds — for some reason I counted silently. Underneath the plaid shirt her skin was warm. She gulped her wine and slid off her stool.

"I have to go," she said as she left, obviously frightened. Frightened of wanting me, I was sure. She had to feel it too.

"It's okay," I tried to reassure her from across the room. Her new jeans fit snugly across her rounded rear. "Come back anytime," I added, hoping she heard me as she slipped out the door.

Larry and Dave were looking at me strangely when I turned back. Feeling unsteady, I went into the back office and sat on the cool leather sofa, running a wet glass of ice cubes over my face. It had started.

CHAPTER FOUR

"Larry told me your straight friend was in the bar last night," Anne announced when I came into the kitchen Saturday morning. I wished I'd checked more carefully that she was gone before leaving my room; I was still avoiding her.

Rob's room was definitely mine now. I missed the waterbed. Radar padded over and I gave her a good pat — more for my own reassurance of being loved than my dog's.

"Aren't you opening the clinic today?" I asked. I didn't want to give any response to her comment about my "straight friend." I suspected I wasn't going to get off any too easily this morning. And I deserved whatever I would get.

"I've got a new tech who's terrific," Anne said, pouring herself raisin bran. "She's opening for me — my first appointment's not for half an hour. Her name's Cheeka, in case you ever call me at the clinic again."

I hadn't called her in weeks. Months? And so what? We were officially broken up, even if we did have this weird financial and living arrangement going. "Was I supposed to have called you?"

"No, of course not, don't be ridiculous. We're doing just fine. Though I did call my attorney and my tax planner to figure out the financial arrangements."

Even though I'd asked for the consultations, I got a chill. Bring in the big guns and you never know what they'll do.

"My tax preparer yelled at me years ago for combining our money," Anne said, going through some papers. "She warned me back then that one day I'd regret it. She's having a heck of a time sorting our money out. But we're not in too bad shape." She showed me where to sign on new bank cards.

"She's my tax preparer too," I said pointedly. "Maybe I should call her?"

"Maybe you should," Anne agreed. "I trust you, but you can never tell what'll happen in the heat of passion. Larry said your straight friend looked nice enough."

"Appearances can be deceiving," I muttered. I was annoyed Anne had brought all this up, though at the same time I had to admit her common sense and money knowledge were among her better points. Without her, I'd have never gotten a business on my own.

I signed some checks for the utilities and assorted home and business mortgages, my sloppy scrawl barely fitting onto the lines while Anne's neat cursive curled underneath.

"That's it," Anne said cheerily, moving to the sink to rinse out her dish. "Oh, and I told the bank to drop our limit so neither of us can take out more than a hundred dollars a day from the automatic teller. That's okay, isn't it?"

"Do I have a choice?"

Anne's hands stopped under the gushing water. After a cool second she turned off the faucet and faced me, fury in her eyes. "You had a choice. You made it."

I had no answer to that. My gaze dropped first. I was being punished, and I deserved it. Though I'd tried to do the honorable thing.

Anne finished the dishes in silence and stacked them neatly before leaving the room. I sat back dully in the hard kitchen chair. It was really final; we were going through with it. No turning back now.

And what if Rhonda never returned? I was on my own, all right. Just the way I wanted it, all right.

Anne left for the clinic and I read the *Times* over coffee. I was out of frozen dinners and a few necessities, and I was in the mood for a walk to clear my mind. I used to jog around the Silverlake reservoir four mornings a week, before my sedentary old ways caught up with me. This would be a good day to start up again.

In cut-offs and T-shirt, Radar at my side, I ran down the winding hillside drive to the lake and kept on toward Mayfair supermarket. I was gasping and choking by then.

With an armful of groceries I made the trek uphill a lot more slowly. Winded, again gasping for breath, I resolved to jog more faithfully. I was painfully aware of what a forty-eight-year-old body might look like to someone twenty years younger. I added a few push-ups to my morning's regime.

Before going to work I drove to the Glendale Galleria for a few new shirts and pairs of slacks. It was too hot for leather jackets to be on display yet. Almost as an afterthought, I bought new underwear from the Broadway. At least that credit card was in my name.

The damage done, I thought about what I had spent and drew out a hundred dollars from an ATM. Having to think seriously about money again was going to be a drag.

I dressed carefully in a black cotton shirt and white pleated slacks, with new black high-tops. All night long I tried to look nonchalant, keeping my eyes away from the door for at least ten seconds at a time.

"You're looking for someone, hey?" Carmen teased. I couldn't deny it.

"Trouble between you and Anne?" she pried.

"Nothing serious," I mumbled. At her cocked head I had to add, "We've broken up, is all."

"You're not going to sell the bar, are you?" Well, of course, Carmen would be concerned about her job. She wasn't really prying.

"I'll be buying Anne out, that's all. Don't worry, you still have a job here as long as you want. You're the one who really runs the place."

"And don't you forget it," Carmen quipped, obvious relief in her eyes. "I'll tell Nancy when she gets here." That was my job, but my heart wasn't in it. Carmen did indeed run the place. The chunky Honduran-born woman went back to work with more spring in her step, while I resolved to not look at the door again.

At nine Rhonda appeared, heading directly to the empty seat nearest to me. I brought her white wine and waved to Carmen to take over while I sat down.

"I'm glad you came," I said.

She smiled and sipped from her glass.

"Last night was my turn to talk. Tonight you get to tell me about yourself."

Instead she darted out of her seat to the jukebox and inserted a handful of coins. It would be a few minutes until her selections came up; the bar was already jammed, and selections had been made before hers. I saw Nancy take my place behind the counter.

Rhonda had on the tight new jeans again, with a pale yellow scoop-neck T-shirt, a yellow print scarf keeping her hair back and off her forehead. The style pointed up the roundness of her face, a perfect circle except for a determined chin that jutted forward as she battled through the crowd. I envied the bodies jostling against her as she made her way across the dance floor.

"What do you want to know about me?" she asked, almost coyly, when she returned.

"Everything," I smiled. She sipped more wine as I waited.

"Okay, I'll start at the beginning. I was born in Horseshoe, a little town in eastern Pennsylvania you never heard of. My father was a farmer and my mother had babies — six of them. When I got out of high school I went to Philadelphia to enroll in nursing school and was assigned to the Episcopalian hospital there, where I met my husband. His family's old money — Bucks County, Pennsylvania and San Marino. He's an Episcopalian priest, graduated from Harvard Divinity School, an old family tradition."

I didn't want to hear any more about her husband, but she went on. "He was assigned to the hospital himself as part of a course in counseling the sick and for a course in medical ethics. I was taking care of a twelve-year-old boy in a coma whose parents wanted to withdraw life support, and I guess I got pretty attached to the kid. So did Charles." She stopped, a smile lighting her face. "The boy's family hated me," she said, barely able to keep from laughing aloud. Finally she couldn't help it — she chuckled, a full-throated sound that made me want to nuzzle her neck.

Michael Jackson's "I'm Bad" came on the jukebox. "Come on, I played that," she said, tugging me on the arm. She did a whole-body shimmy like my mother used to do when she showed me the Charleston from her own "flapper" days. Would Rhonda know what a flapper was? She shimmied again to get me off my chair. I had to laugh.

We forced our way onto the dance floor and

moved around as best we could. I wanted to order everyone to clear out so I could see her playful moves, lipsynching "I'm bad" like a mischievous child with an angelic face.

But then I silently thanked the crowds when she was shoved up against me, her hand grabbing me around the waist to catch herself, her red-gold hair flinging back against my cheek like a kitten's soft tail. I grabbed her too, to steady her, my hands digging into her waist, her body taut beneath her clothes.

We stood there, holding each other for a long second, while the music changed and couples came and went from the floor. Her body burned against mine.

She broke away first. I followed her to our seats and shooed away the couple who had stolen them.

Rhonda gulped the rest of her wine. "I can't stay long tonight," she said. "Charles has an important sermon to give tomorrow — the bishop and some other rectors will be there — and he asked me to help him rehearse. Usually he locks himself up in his study Saturday nights with all his fancy video equipment and writes his sermons and rehearses them on tape until he's happy with them. Sometimes he doesn't finish until dawn."

"That's why you come by on Saturday nights," I guessed.

She made a deliberate pout. "I want to be here a lot more. Don't you know that?" She reached out and let her hand rest on my neck. I could feel a rush of blood.

I wanted to believe that she did, too.

"I was able to sneak out for a little while last night, remember."

I did.

"Next week he'll be away at a conference all weekend. I'm coming by Friday night and we can spend some time together," she whispered. "I'll see you then." She gathered her purse and left two dollars for the wine and made her way out the door. I watched her in those jeans until she was out of sight.

It had happened so fast I could barely comprehend it — one moment we were in each other's arms, the next she was gone. That was just how she was, I decided ruefully.

Had she implied she'd be free all next weekend? My mind raced through the possibilities.

In a fog, I went back behind the bar and poured a few for some of my favorite customers. Already tongues would be wagging in the community. People were used to not seeing Anne, but they weren't used to seeing me looking like a fool, tongue hanging out, panting for another woman.

To hell with them all. Rhonda was worth it.

I was restless for the remainder of the evening. Finally I retreated to the back office and looked through the area phone books, on the off chance I'd see her listed. I had a whole shelf for L.A. and vicinity phone books. In San Marino I looked up Churches, Episcopal.

There it was: Christ the King, San Marino, Dr. Charles H. Rasmussen, Rector. Services at nine a.m. and eleven a.m., Sunday school at ten a.m.

Under individual listings in the white pages I

found the home address for Charles H. Rasmussen. Surprise, it was next to the church.

When I got home it was already four a.m. I set the alarm for eight and tossed in the single bed for the next four hours.

CHAPTER FIVE

I should try driving Sundays at eight more often — it took only half an hour to get there.

Christ the King was a gothic monstrosity. I was raised Roman Catholic, more or less, in the early years when my mother was living at home and feeling good about herself. I never did like the cold gray flying buttresses and heavy stone columns of old cathedrals. But it fit its surroundings in San Marino, one of the richest communities in the U.S.

I felt an unexpected tug to go inside and take part in the service. Huh, where did that come from?

Maybe thinking about church brought back the good memories about my mother, when she was still around. I shook off the thoughts. My mother was long gone, who knew where?

The parsonage next door looked like an English country manor — ivy covering much of the stone and brick frontage, a massive stone chimney, neatly trimmed hedges and walkways. A rose garden could be seen down one path.

I parked on the street in my Chevy S-10, the blue pickup definitely out of place among the Beemers, Jags and Rolls Royces. I was just in time.

At 8:35 Rhonda and a tall man in a white clerical gown left the parsonage and walked to the church to greet early parishioners. Rhonda wore a white linen suit and beige pumps, a beige and peach floral scarf at her neckline. Her hair was off her neck, a French braid keeping it close to the back of her head, loose curls on top, two long curls like wings framing her face. Plain white pearl buttons accented her ears. She was even more beautiful in this formal setting. Princess Grace reigning over Monaco.

She smiled at everyone and welcomed them with confident handshakes while her husband stood more stiffly beside her. Her husband seemed relieved to finally go inside. Another couple joined Rhonda, official greeters of some sort. Then everyone entered the church. A grand organ began to play, audible even to me outside.

I debated joining the congregation, sitting inconspicuously in the back, but from the way everyone seemed to know one another, and the way they were dressed, there might be a rustling or whisper that could cause Rhonda to look back and spot me. Or were Episcopalians too formal to fidget, even at the sight of a tousle-haired, six-foot dyke in T-shirt and jeans?

It was kind of like the huge Catholic churches I used to attend with my mother — when her face wasn't too badly bruised — where everyone knew their place and their duties and they followed their dress code as faithfully as a commandment — maybe more faithfully. This crowd did discreet nods in one another's direction, probably the most enthusiasm they showed all day.

I envisioned Rhonda in the first-row pew, sitting sweetly in her place, the model minister's wife. Then I remembered her teasing dancing last night to "I'm Bad." Little did the congregation know.

She seemed to fit in this life, just as she had fit into Samms'. A chameleon. Maybe she could get away with living two totally contradictory lives. Maybe she'd be one of those lesbians who always stayed in their upper-class straight life, playing at being a lesbian only when hubby's away. I didn't think I could take being the lover of someone like that. I didn't like the fact Rhonda went home to this man after leaving me.

He was a homely sort, tall and thin and ramrod-spined, all angles. His nondescript, short brown hair had a thick hank dead center above his forehead that would have fallen in his eyes, given half a chance to grow or a cheaper haircut. Horn-rimmed glasses made him look austere. Dr. Rasmussen. He looked ten years older than Rhonda.

I drove off thinking about this side of Rhonda's life. He wasn't even good-looking. But maybe she'd needed a straight-arrow kind of guy, just as I'd needed Anne.

Or maybe she'd married him for money. It was okay with me if she had. If her family was poor, she might have grasped any opportunity to get away. And maybe she didn't want to leave all this luxury. Not all priests took a vow of poverty, it was clear. What drove Rhonda to marry this man, if not money? And was she being driven *to* me, or away from him, and why? What were her ambitions, her goals? Where was she heading? And was there room for me? Did I want to make room for her?

I examined my own role. Having left Anne, was I doomed to repeat my one-night-stand days, willing to drift until I happened to land next to someone drifting my same direction? Was it just sexual attraction on both our parts, and if so, was that okay in this day and age? Seeing her next to the minister convinced me I needn't worry about AIDS with her—he wasn't the cheating type. Maybe one-night stands didn't deserve their bad rap — didn't every relationship start with what might be a one-night stand?

If I kept up this fantasizing and imagining, I could make myself sick. Only she could tell me more about herself. Only time would tell if there was more than sexual attraction going between us. I drove back to L.A. and went to the bar early, then crashed on the sofabed until opening.

All week long I waited for Friday night. I came up with an angle that practically guaranteed AIDS Aid would get the new grant, which made me a hero at Monday night's meeting. That helped my self-image, which was a little quivery at the moment.

When she arrived, I almost didn't recognize her. She had on a white wrap skirt in a kind of light jersey, a white top arranged in some way so that it was backless clear to the waistline, a teal blue and gold-striped cummerbund, and a long gold scarf that made a sort of hood.

Her face was half-hidden by the gold hood; she caught me by surprise when she sauntered up to the bar and asked, "Where's my white wine?" The hood fell off to show her hair plaited with golden yellow baby rosebuds. Her round face glowed pink like a bride's. The same face that greeted parishioners. When would the "I'm Bad" face show itself?

Fumbling with her drink, I wanted to reach across the bar and kiss her. From the vibes I was getting, my fantasies just might come true. I dismissed them immediately as unrealistic. This was a minister's wife, a babydyke, an innocent. I'd slept with women without knowing a thing about them. But this was no typical one-night stand. I'd have to go slow. I definitely wanted her. My chest caught when I tried to breathe.

I whisked her away to a table in a corner and took off the "Reserved" sign. "You look beautiful," I whispered.

"Thank you."

For a moment neither of us said anything. I could feel my breasts tingling against my rough-woven natural cotton safari jacket. I'd left off a bra — never did have much to support anyway.

A Mariah Carey ballad came on the jukebox. Without a word we got up and began to dance. My hand rested against her bare skin in the backless top. Her skin was soft and warm. I could feel my palm perspiring and I discreetly wiped my hand against my slacks before touching her again.

She tucked her head under my chin, the flowers tickling my nose. Her perfume intensified the roses. I felt dizzy and had to concentrate on my feet, though we didn't dance so much as sway, my hand pressing against her body, her head against my breast. Her breathing penetrated my shirt, each breath a flutter of a breeze through the cotton.

A memory of her standing so self-assured at her husband's side greeting parishioners broke through. Should I tell her I'd seen her at the church? No, she'd think I was spying, which is exactly what I'd done.

I could feel my mouth nudging at her, trying to get her to turn her face upward. I couldn't just hold her to me any longer, or I'd do something premature. Abruptly I led her back to the table and sat down. She followed.

Nancy delivered my Diet Pepsi and another white wine for her, without our asking. I drained mine and signaled for another. Briefly I wished it were a white Russian instead. Never cured, just one day at a time. One moment at a time. One sentence at a time.

"Tell me more about yourself, Rhonda." Saying her name was like breathing a proposition. She looked so happy and excited. The image kept coming up: like a bride. The scent of roses made me giddy. I sat up straight and took a deep breath, forcing myself to scan the crowd.

It was a busy night. One of the young women from the softball team I sponsor was drunk, falling all over herself and others on the dance floor, using a chair for a partner since apparently no one would dance with her. A chair leg threatened another dancer's eye. My star hitter. She caught my glare and cooled it, at least for the moment. I'd 86 her soon, even if she did threaten to quit the team again.

"What do you want to know?" There was the tease again.

How soon can I get you into bed? No, couldn't say that. I mentally slapped myself. "Anything you want to tell me. First, one question — are you a dancer?"

She laughed. "I always wanted to be a ballerina when I was a kid, but there wasn't any dance school in Horseshoe, even if we could afford it. So a couple of years ago I discovered a ballet school in Pasadena that takes adult beginners. It's my daily exercise to keep in shape. But I'm hardly a dancer."

"I wouldn't say that. When you were working out to 'I'm Bad' last time, could have fooled me. So what else do you like?"

She sat back in the wooden chair. "Oh, I like rain, and snow. Lawns that grow green all by themselves. Streams. I miss Pennsylvania. But I love the ocean and mountains, which is why I still love L.A. I like swimming and hiking. I like all kinds of music — Gloria Estefan, the old Karen Carpenter songs. Ten Thousand Maniacs." Looking embarrassed, she paused. "I hate to admit it, but I like Michael Jackson, even though he's supposed to be passé. He's so insecure he just cries out for mothering, which is why people don't respect him any more. I'd like to see him sing 'Sometimes I Feel Like a Motherless Child' some day — I bet he couldn't get through it, and I'd like to be there to comfort him and help him get himself together again."

Good grief, maybe she was younger than I thought. I forced myself to smile. Shades of adolescence.

"Let's see, what else. Georgia O'Keeffe. Rosebuds . . ."

I listened. The part of me that was paying attention wanted to mother that part of her that identified with Michael Jackson's vulnerability. No, what I felt wasn't mothering. I reached out and tugged one of the yellow rosebuds from her braid. A tuft of hair came loose with the flower. The ceiling fans puffed it free.

"So far we have a few things in common," I finally said, when she stopped talking. It was obviously my turn. This seemed like first-date chatter. High school dating. The kind I never did.

"Now you," she insisted.

Um, this was going to be hard. "Okay, thunderstorms. We don't get them enough in L.A."

"Me too!" She waited for more.

What else could I say? "I have a German Shepherd named Radar. She looks vicious but she's a sweetheart."

She let me off the hook with only two items and went on to describe every dog she had ever owned, followed by every singer she had ever enjoyed. I never heard of half of them, and I consider myself fairly up on the music world because of the huge jukebox at the bar.

It wasn't until she started to list her favorite foods that I could get into it. We went through an imaginary twelve-course dinner that rivaled the film *Tom Jones*. We were off at the Santa Monica Pier riding the merry-go-round before we dared to dance again.

Carmen interrupted us with obvious reluctance. I had a phone call. I tugged Rhonda along with me to the back office to take it, even though the portable phone I keep on the desk sometimes doesn't make a connection and the batteries wear down. It was charged this time.

Rhonda looked around with interest as I urged the Stonewall Democratic Club's chairperson, who was returning my earlier call, to do a joint fundraiser with AIDS Aid, and maybe a joint mailing. Okay, so I wasn't totally incompetent as an organizer without Anne's direction — that was good to realize. As I talked, I could feel Rhonda's amusement at the tiny sink, stove and refrigerator.

I'd cleaned up the place, changed the sofabed linens to fresh blue-striped sheets, washed the curtains, stocked juice in the fridge, put away the papers on the desk. Just in case. What a presumptuous dreamer.

"Do you live here?" she asked when I hung up.

"Sometimes. The previous owner did."

She came over in front of me and put her arms around my neck. Her soft kiss sent electricity through me so strongly I thought I'd catch fire. Spontaneous combustion. I could read the supermarket tabloids now: "Dyke Kisses Priest's Wife, Erupts in Flames."

Rhonda released me and stood there, watching me. She let a slow smile spread over her face.

Reaching again, she kissed me on the nose and immediately tugged me toward the door leading to the bar.

"You've got a bar to run, Ms. Silly Samms," she said, her eyes playing grays and greens and blues like a Pacific sunrise. Mischievously she pulled me out the door. I straightened my shirt and headed back to our table, evicting the squatters from our chairs. The noise was too loud.

"I can't hear you, let's go back into the apartment," I said. She gave me a questioning look. *So soon,* I almost heard her ask, *with all these people on the other side of the door?*

"I really do want to talk," I insisted. "I don't want everybody to know our business any more than you do."

That did it. I left the table to the squatters and we headed back into the apartment, picking up wine and Pepsi as we went. I was careful to sit at the desk while Rhonda chose the sofabed.

"So tell me, Ms. Samms, are you seeing any women right now?"

The direct question caught me by surprise. "All I see is you. Seriously, I broke off with the veterinarian I mentioned. I'm not seeing anyone and haven't been with anyone else besides her in nineteen years. It was a long relationship but it's over." I paused. "Are you faithful to your husband?"

"Since the day we met," she replied promptly.

"Unless you count lusting in your heart?"

"What?"

"Remember Jimmy Carter told *Playboy* that . . . never mind." She would have been in grade school, maybe junior high. I was really getting old. She gave me a forgiving smile anyway. Was she lusting right now? She had to be. One sentence at a time. "So who did you lust after before you got up your courage to come here?"

She glanced away.

"Come now, out of the blue you didn't suddenly decide you might be attracted to women. What woman first turned you on?"

"Oh, all right," she said, concentrating on her wine glass. "Don't laugh, there's a woman in the choir. She's . . . so alive. I just found myself staring at her all the time and getting . . . excited."

"So why aren't you with her instead of me?" I was jealous to the core of my being but I wouldn't show it.

"Oh, she's happily married. *Very* happily. She loves her husband so much you can just see it She hangs all over him, and he's all over her. They're the scandal of San Marino — even newlyweds aren't supposed to show all that sexuality. She just oozes it, but it's all for him." Rhonda's eyes were bright.

"So I'm second-best, the stand-in."

Rhonda reached across the desk and patted my hand. "I'm not stupid, I wasn't going to keep longing after an impossible dream. I have to thank her, really, for making me see something about myself. I always did kind of like my girlfriends more than boys. You should see Charles. He's a good man but he's absolutely the least sexy man you've ever seen."

I kept myself from saying, "I know." Instead I asked, "How do you explain to your husband why you're gone so much?" I wouldn't pursue any more questions about this choir singer; no sense driving myself nuts over it. So what if she'd been attracted to another woman first? I should be grateful to this unknown, happily married competitor.

"I don't give him any explanations. He likes to think he's a feminist. He wouldn't dare question me, though he wants to. I know he's jealous, and it embarrasses him."

"Doesn't he even ask questions?"

Rhonda laughed. "He probably imagines the worst, but it would be beneath his dignity to do anything about it. I told you, he's busy every Saturday night rehearsing sermons, and he goes to a lot of meetings. Episcopalians like meetings."

"Aren't you supposed to be alongside him, the pastor's dutiful wife and all that?"

"Oh, sometimes I am. Parishes more or less put up with the pastor's wife. They don't want too much of me. I'd love to take over the sick calls for Charles, and with my nursing background I'd be good at it. But the rich biddies getting plastic surgery at Huntington Memorial want their pastor. He tries to hide it but he can't stand sickness."

"The counseling course didn't help him?"

Her eyes quizzed me. "Oh, the one at the hospital where we met. No, not really. I can't imagine he gives anybody much comfort. He's in his glory making some intellectual sermon that impresses everyone and inspires no one. And that's what the Episcopalians of San Marino seem to want."

"No rousing calls to action?" Actually I was more interested in her eyes. "I've never been to a Protestant church — all I've seen are the TV evangelists, I guess."

"Charles is nothing like that." Rhonda frowned.

"Jealous though. He would never show it, but I know he is. He just closes up and doesn't face it. He has to know something's up. I tell him I have to lead my own life, enjoy my own pursuits. He knows I wasn't cut out to be a priest's wife. I suspect he even knows I hate it."

"Why don't you leave?" I met her eyes directly, challenging her. This was an important question for me.

"Don't you think I've thought about it? I would in a second, except it might ruin his career. Priests have careers too, you know. He's no selfless good Samaritan. He's in it for the glory just like the rest of his family. He just wears a different collar doing it. And boy, does that family run him. Nobody in his entire family has ever gotten a divorce, they wouldn't dare, that's how much control Daddy exerts. It's worse than royalty."

I didn't want to know anything more about Daddy. Or hubby, either, but Rhonda seemed to need to talk about him.

"He's risen pretty high pretty fast, thanks to all the right connections. He was called to a nice church in Bucks County right away. And then with his family in San Marino he was able to get this calling when he was only thirty-three. That was four years ago. I doubt if they'd kick him out if he got divorced, even if it never came out why I left, but he wouldn't be seen in quite the same way, if you know what I mean." She smiled. "His next assignment might be ... " She struggled for an appropriately come-down spot.

"Cucamonga," I said, remembering how the conductor on the old Jack Benny shows used to read off all the funny names of towns outside L.A., with Cucamonga being the most remote as well as the funniest sounding.

"Where?"

She was too young to remember Jack Benny. "Timbuktu," I offered instead.

"Huh?"

"Never mind." I felt even older. I decided to ask the biggie: "What about his money?"

I was glad she looked offended. Then she shrugged. "I was eighteen when we met. I was six months out of high school, washing bedpans and trying to learn chemistry, when I met this guy who seemed so smart, so sophisticated. We kept finding ourselves next to each other at the bedside of this little boy in a coma, and I could tell he fell for me. Finally we started going out. He called me his Botticelli cherub. I'd never heard of Botticelli."

I grimaced. So I wasn't the first to think her round face called out for angelic descriptions.

"My family was never all that supportive of me. I was in the middle of six kids and kind of got lost a lot."

That was hard for me to picture. I told her so. I was intrigued by her every word, watching how her eyes changed from green to gold to dark turquoise to shadowy blue to almost hazy gray-brown, whenever the light hitting her face shifted.

She snickered. "Believe me, I wasn't particularly good-looking as a kid. This hair could only be controlled in pigtails, and I was overweight and freckly."

"I don't see any freckles."

"You won't see me without makeup, either."

"I like freckles." I squinted, trying to see any spots on her nose.

"Then maybe you'll see me without makeup someday."

"I hope so."

We sipped our drinks.

"I'm not saying I won't miss the money. I'd feel better if it were my own, that I earned with my own efforts, not money that his family made screwing miners."

"That's where the money comes from?"

"Something related to mining. Just about everything in Pennsylvania goes back to mining. Anyway, his family was scared to death that I was after his money, and his father's lawyers drew up a prenuptial agreement. I signed it, no big thing. It never felt like the money was mine anyway."

She looked into an imaginary distance, or a very-real past, I couldn't tell which.

"Laney, this probably sounds funny, but I don't want to hurt him. I don't want there to be some big scandal — can you see *The National Enquirer* — 'Priest's Wife Is a Dyke'?"

I smiled with her, remembering my own made-up headlines of a moment before. "So you don't think anybody from Christ the King is likely to be in Silverlake drinking at Samms'?"

"How did you know his church is Christ the King?"

I was flustered, then admitted, "I looked it up. In the phone book. I just wanted to know more about you."

She didn't look irritated, only pleased. "I thought about being seen — I thought about it a lot. Then I figured that anyone who saw me here would be gay too, and they'd be hiding out too. So I'd be safe."

"You're probably right. When I was first coming out I looked up 'homosexual' in the New York phone books. Nothing. But this was a long time ago, remember." I shook my head at the memory. Times had changed — we'd had to fight for the right to use the words *gay* and *lesbian* in phone listings. "Finally I tracked down a women's bar in the Village. I was home. But one night something terrifying happened — I looked across the room and spotted my sergeant! Before I could split, she saw me too. She was more scared than I was — she had more to lose. We got together right after that."

I smiled at the memories. I'd been in my leather jacket ensemble, Gladys had worn a red rayon dress and black patent leather heels, a far cry from her Army uniform. I learned how to play butch to her femme real fast, even to the point of never asking for sexual satisfaction for myself, supposedly content only to pleasure her. That was one of the lies butches told ourselves back then. I certainly was not into that part of the role any more. I chuckled aloud.

Rhonda laughed too, apparently at her own memories. "I found this place from a flyer at Page One bookstore in Pasadena. It seemed far enough away that no one would see me, yet close enough that I wouldn't get lost. I get lost a lot in L.A."

There was that motherless child look again. I wanted to comfort her. "Everybody does, you can't help it. So . . ." I paused and asked another biggie: "What are you going to do about your marriage?"

She looked down. "I hate to say this, but I don't want to leave my husband until I'm sure . . ."

"Sure you're a lesbian?" I finished for her after another lengthy pause.

She looked grateful. "Does that make me a terrible person?'"

"No."

"But I'm not sure how to do that."

"Looks to me like you do. And you're doing it." I gave her what was supposed to be my most supportive smile. She trembled. I changed the subject. "When did you first find out what lesbianism is?"

"I remember having a crush on a girl in grade school, and one day on the playground this other girl started talking about the Isle of Lesbos and all those terrible women. I knew right away somehow that I was one of those terrible women. So with a vengeance, I started going after boys to prove I wasn't."

For some reason the incident seemed almost familiar. But then our coming-out stories all seem to include some such memory in adolescence. I tried picturing her as a freckle-faced overweight child. She must have been adorable even then.

"And then when we first got to L.A., there was a woman in our parish who suddenly started bringing another woman to church with her. They looked like I thought lesbians looked — short, straight, boring hair, jeans and workshirts, comfortable shoes . . ."

I tucked my Reeboks under the table.

"Everybody started to talk about them, especially when they moved in together. They left the church right after that, and I don't blame them. Last I heard they were going to a big gay church in downtown L.A."

"Metropolitan Community Church," I acknowledged.

"I heard there was an Episcopal gay group, too."

"Yeah. Dignity, I think. No, that's the Catholics. Oh, it's called Integrity."

She nodded. "And then one day I was looking at the woman in the choir, and I remembered how the gay couple had to leave our church and I got real scared."

I remembered the feeling, the first day I thought I was different. I told her more about my coming out, and about other women who had gone through tough times coming out.

"You know, Laney, the one thing I don't understand is how a woman can leave her children to become gay. You'd think she would hold out until the kids were older, teenagers anyway."

I hadn't thought much about the ethics of staying together for the sake of the kids. Anne's boy was in medical school at Stanford now, and he'd been an infant when she left her husband. I knew from the start Rob would be a part of our lives, and it was no big deal for me, though we'd all had to go to counseling for a while. When he was about twelve and finally realized who and what I was, he'd started making grunting sounds at the dinner table and resisting everything I said. He came around.

I have to admit, I got jealous sometimes when she put him first over me. But I understood. It was one of the things I'd loved about her. I didn't want to tell Rhonda about all that. It hinted at too much closeness, too much shared history, between Anne and me.

"I mean, raising a child is an important obligation. You can't just give away a kid like you can a kitten," she insisted. "No matter how much you'd like to be doing something else, you don't dump a kid."

I assured her that the decision wouldn't be easy for any lesbian who did leave her children with her ex-husband or family. I began to wonder why she was so concerned about the issue of children. "Do you have any kids?"

She visibly paled, makeup or not. I thought she would cry on the spot. "No, we tried. I wanted kids a lot. I went to all the doctors, and they told me I'd gotten an infection from an IUD and couldn't conceive. Then I went through an operation to open my fallopian tubes. That didn't work either. We even tried the test tube route, but it doesn't work for everybody. We popped five grand a month to USC for six months. Nothing."

We were silent. She was clearly upset.

She continued finally, "We talked about adoption. We're even on a waiting list. I guess that's out now."

This time she did sniffle, tears tracking her cheeks. "Excuse me," she said. "I have to use the restroom. And I can't use this one." It was right there, visible from the desk, in this crowded, one room office-apartment. "Maybe we should go back outside. They'll be missing you."

The moment was over. She left and I headed for the bar.

"Is everything all right, Laney?" Carmen asked.

"Thanks, yeah, things are fine. We just hit a sensitive topic, that's all."

"Look, Laney, I hate to pry, but how are things with you and Anne? I haven't seen her — are you still talking?"

"Carmen, I told you, we're okay about this. We'll still own the bar together, you still have your job, I'll probably buy Anne out over the next few years. Our accountant's working on it. Don't worry, we'll be fine."

"Okay if you say so. Your new friend sure is pretty." Carmen winked at me. I felt like a teenage male in the locker room.

I looked over to see what my rowdy softball player was up to. She'd quieted down. Carmen followed my eyes. "I threatened to bounce her and she shut up. She's on ginger ale right now."

"Good. Say, if things keep this busy, call in Tim to help out the last couple of hours."

Tim lives two houses down the side street and we call on him a lot as a bouncer and bartender. He tested positive a few years back and doesn't go out much, so he's usually home on a Saturday night. I've tried to encourage him to get out more but he prefers to stay in. It's my gain, having a temp within hailing distance.

"Sure, good idea." She winked at me again as she left. A big macho wink. I always hated her winking. Carmen had been in this country almost as long as Samms' had been open; we'd been her first and only job. A terrific bartender, she learned perfect English in Honduras and sometimes corrects my grammar, but she'd picked up some of the worst gestures. If I did buy out the bar maybe I'd give her a promotion. And I'd give her a righteous dressing-down on how that sort of wink was mainly used by crude men to demean women.

As I burned inside at the memory of that wink, my face heated — the film of Max and me Anne had taken twenty years ago when I was last drunk had shown me giving just such a wink to a prospective one-night stand. No wonder it bugged me. So it was my problem, not Carmen's.

Rhonda was back, her face red from an apparent scrubbing. Freckles showed through this time. She must have seen me staring at them; she pointed to her nose and grinned. I could see the pigtailed child this time.

"Sorry I got so shook up," she apologized. "I really wanted to have a baby. Now that I'm thinking about ways to leave Charles, I'm finally admitting it won't happen."

Carefully, I said, "Someday you might find yourself in a relationship with a woman who has children, and then you'll get to raise them too."

She looked startled. "I'd never thought about that. I guess lesbians with children have love-lives too. How do the kids take it?"

"Every kid is different. Most make a pretty good adjustment, same as any kid with a stepparent."

She digested the idea. "Maybe I'll have to read some more at Page One. I was shocked to see all the gay books."

"Ummm. Good store." The conversation drifted off as we watched others dance, waiting for a song that would grab us. I reached across the table and took her hands in mine.

There went the jingling sensation again. I felt like jumping out of my seat and shaking my body all over to get rid of it, like a kid who just stuck her finger into an electrical outlet.

As I rubbed her hands in mine the jolts mellowed out, as if finding their own niche in my hungry nervous system.

CHAPTER SIX

For the rest of the night we danced. Tim came in to help Carmen and Nancy with the bartending, leaving me to be the subject of nods and nudges all night.

Carmen apparently filled Tim in, with her own version of all this. I didn't care. I'd been honest with Anne. I'd kept up my responsibility. People would adjust — I'd seen the community adjust to incredible changes in my lifetime. And so would Anne.

Again I regretted that a thought of her had

slipped in, while I held Rhonda as closely as I dared and swam in the light scent of roses.

As the night wore on I could feel Rhonda letting herself nestle into my arms, into my body. With each fast song she let go a little more, trying more moves, even a rap hip-hop that made her giggle. The ballet training showed. With each slow song her arms slipped around my neck more easily, more tightly.

Billy Joel came on the jukebox with another oldie, "For the Longest Time." True, I hadn't felt this way for the longest time. Maybe never. Rhonda was special.

Priest's wife. I nearly choked. *Discovering her sexuality.* I forced the thoughts away.

My hands crept by inches, exploring the way her waist indented under the teal and gold cummerbund and the curves down toward her hips. The deep back vee of her white blouse led my fingers onto her soft back, her skin taut over her small frame, beads of perspiration spreading into a dewy film as my fingertips reached them.

I tried to ask more questions. "Don't." She stopped me with a fingertip to my lips. I nibbled on the fingertip. She smiled and let herself be kissed.

As I opened my eyes and drew back I caught a glimpse of Tim, disapproving. He shook his head, then caught himself and smiled an innocent smile. Employees don't criticize their boss's private life, at least not blatantly, I could see him telling himself.

That's right, and don't you forget it. I sent the silent message across the room, before letting my attention slide back to Rhonda.

"Last call," I heard someone say. Startled, I

looked at the clock. Ten to two. Meaning it was really a little after one-thirty, a trick every bar owner uses to get dawdlers out on time, though since everybody knows it's standard practice, no one pays much attention.

I pulled back from Rhonda's arms and made a stab at closing the bar, though Carmen and crew were obviously in charge. My head was spinning. I couldn't think. I didn't know what to do next.

Tim gave me a condescending look as he took a damp rag out of my helpless hands and cleaned off the tables as couples straggled out to the rear garden. Rhonda stood quietly in the shadows, keeping her eyes discreetly lowered. I wondered if she'd caught the suspicious, even hostile glances that more than once had come our way. Or, like me, didn't she care?

Was she as confused, as uncertain, as I was at this moment? Desperately needing to keep her in my arms, not wanting to let her go, all the while knowing it was too soon, much too soon?

That had never stopped me in the past — I'd been the queen of one-night stands in my younger days. At this exact moment of the evening when the bars were closing, I'd be frantic to find someone who would spend the night with me. To keep my loneliness at bay, I had to prove to myself that I was okay, despite the overwhelming sense that I would never be a good person, that I didn't deserve a good relationship, that my father's drunken tirades at me were justified.

One therapist had made me feel like an answering machine: simply replace the messages you tell yourself with new messages to make yourself feel better. I put on a new tape: I am a worthwhile, responsible, loving human being. I don't have to act out of desperation. All I have to do is to take a deep breath and think what is the right thing to do, then do it. I am in charge of my own life. My higher power will make it possible.

My higher power sometimes comes off like a smartass. "You got yourself into this mess, now get yourself out of it. Send her home to hubby. Take a hike." I told HP to take a hike. I was on my own.

I should put Rhonda back in her yellow convertible and get the hell out of her life. Let her screw around with her new-found lesbianism on her own for a few months, a few years, then see what she was like. Don't take advantage of her at this vulnerable moment, I told myself. Don't go with raw body heat. You're being totally stupid. Brain, take charge.

The last customer left the bar and Tim turned out the lights on us. "Good night, you two," he smirked, then caught himself again and said, "Good night, Rhonda, it was nice meeting you tonight. Good night, Laney. Have a good evening, or rather, morning. Shall I open up tomorrow?" If there was still any hint of sarcasm there, I couldn't sense it. "Thanks, Tim, I'd appreciate it. I'll be in around noon." Nobody much would be in at ten in the morning since there wasn't a ballgame scheduled to kick off — not that my team's tradition of gathering for an opening beer before a game helped their playing much.

"Don't rush." He left, checking the lock behind him.

"We're alone now," Rhonda said, shivering. The

air conditioner had gone on in response to the doors opening so much in the 2 a.m. rush. She rubbed her bare arms and slid the gold hood up over her hair. Tendrils of red-gold had worked themselves loose throughout the evening, and the yellow rosebuds drooped.

Conscious of where my eyes had strayed, she began to remove the pins which had kept the roses and plaits in her hair. The hood loosened, her hair cascaded in waves to her shoulders. She opened her arms to me and led me into the back room.

I heard a gurgling sound from HP. My higher power was sent on high.

She reached up to kiss me, moving my hands onto her breasts. Wondrous breasts, round and firm, puckered into cool hard nipples under my fingertips. She slid the white top off her shoulders, untied the cummerbund and stepped out of the white skirt, leaving only a lacy half slip.

It came off with her pantyhose in one smooth motion and they were tossed into a corner. Then she unbuttoned my safari jacket and touched my own breasts like petting a kitten. Her eyes were wide-eyed blue when she looked up at me in awe.

"We're really doing it," she breathed. "I've wanted you so much. I'm scared."

"I am, too, a little."

"I don't know what to do," she whispered.

"Don't worry, do whatever you feel like doing. Is this really okay with you? We could wait."

Sure we could wait.

She said no words, just kissed me again and clutched at my breasts with a hard pressure that bordered on pain. I held her arms and loosened them slightly. "I'm sorry, that must have hurt. I wasn't thinking," she apologized, and bent to kiss my nipples, one at a time, seemingly surprised to see them crinkle into hard knots at the touch of her lips. I undid my slacks and let my body join hers.

Hands on each other's breasts, kneading lightly and stroking, leaning into each other's bodies with our full weight so that we held each other up, we kissed for long moments. I tugged her toward the sofa. "It's a bed," I said, reluctantly pulling away.

The mattress frame wouldn't come loose; together we tugged until it popped out of the sofa frame and landed with a plop on the floor. We laughed and flopped on the bed before the mattress could stop rocking. For one moment she caught herself and looked scared again.

"It's not too late to stop," I said softly.

Oh yes, it was.

I could see in her eyes that it cost her something to scoot her body next to mine. The tension was over, the decision made beyond revocation. We wrapped our legs around each other and kissed in abandonment, exploring each other's body in admiration.

The air was chilly. I rolled Rhonda over on her side, following on top of her, and pulled the blue-striped sheets loose to cover us. The fresh smell of cool new sheets was as arousing as her rose perfume.

Slowly I let my hand slip along the damp skin

between her legs, spreading them slightly. She shuddered, then relaxed with a moan.

Once she was comfortable with the feelings of my hand where no woman had ever touched, I slid down along her body and let my tongue explore and find her rhythms and patterns of delight.

Would I ever get enough of that creamy taste, the joys of finding each crevice and crease, of feeling out each pleasurable place and lingering there before reluctantly leaving and searching for more? I hoped not.

She came with a jolt that knocked my head back and caused me to bite my lip, her heaving sending the sofa bed on a two-step walk across the room.

It went on for minutes, one spasm wrenching into the next, while I held her and rocked her and kept my fingers touching her gently. And then she lay still.

She was crying, her sobbing echoing the heaves that had come before. I held her. It had been too soon. Now she would leave. I would pay for this moment. What was running through her mind? I was afraid to know.

She cried into my shoulder, wet skin against wet skin. Her back was drenched. I pulled the sheet over her again to keep her warm. "It's all right," I finally said. "There, there," I whispered. "It's going to be all right."

"Oh, Laney, you've made me so happy."

A great flush of relief swept over me. A long moment passed as her body stilled. Then she raised her head to meet my eyes.

A sheen polished her round face, drops of sweat

glistening in the faint street light through the window. She was illuminated like a translucent Madonna in a 15th-century oil painting.

"You've made me so happy," she repeated. I felt her grow tense again. "Now I want to please you," she said, "and I don't know how."

"Do whatever you've dreamed of doing, do what you feel like and listen to my body and hear what I like best," I told her softly.

She moved awkwardly in the bed and gingerly tried some stroking before letting her tongue follow where it would. My nearly instant orgasm rolled over me like an elephant, crushing my breath and making me gasp in near-pain. A herd of elephants tiptoed on my belly.

I held her tightly and made her stop. I couldn't take another. She lay in my arms and we rocked in the bed, unable to let go. Finally our bodies stilled, and she drifted into sleep.

I lay there in wonderment. Yes, she was a lesbian. Yes, I was a lesbian. Yes, being a lesbian was the greatest gift on earth.

I thought premature thoughts and made premature plans the rest of the night until I somehow fell asleep too and dreamed of making love in grassy meadows and leaping over deep chasms and always making it to the other side, hand in hand with Rhonda.

She awoke first, as the sun shone onto our faces. She was kissing me in real life just as she was kissing me in my dreams, and I allowed my life to drift back into reality to find it was just as pleasant as my sleep world.

"Good morning, Silver," she said, tousling my hair.

"Good morning, darling," I said, reaching for her. A prolonged kiss, then I wrenched myself away to go to the bathroom. She did the same. Hot and sticky, I turned on the shower, knowing she would join me.

My apartment shower was too crowded to engage in all the happy horseplay and loving that the movies always show. We took turns soaping each other and rinsing, and bumping into each other as we attempted to towel dry in the cramped space. Laughing, we returned to the bed.

This time lovemaking was easier, with memories and patterns fresh in our minds, experience making the moment sweeter if somewhat less intense.

This time she came like running deer, darting gracefully from peak to peak, flowing in a stream of fluid body movements.

I couldn't come.

It was morning, I didn't know the time, and Tim was due to open up. What was ahead for us, what would we do now?

"It's okay, Rhonda. I'm just tense all of a sudden. Last night was so wonderful that my body hasn't fully recovered yet. It's okay, really it is."

She seemed to believe me, and she disappeared back into the bathroom with her satchel, to appear in a pair of white dressy shorts, the gold hood now a strapless bandeau, the white blouse with deep vee back of the previous night now turned around into a jacket, the teal and gold cummerbund now a headband.

"What do we do now?" she asked.

"What do you want to do?" Usually I plan things very carefully in a seduction, moving from scene to scene in my mind, planning for all possibilities. I hadn't dared go beyond the seduction this time, though I'd dreamed. I didn't have the faintest idea what came next.

"Maybe we should go for breakfast — I'm famished," she said with a giggle. "You wore me out. Hey, maybe we could go to your place. I'll cook for you. I'm a great cook. I'd love to see where you really live."

She stood there, anticipating, eyes lit, round face shining, tanned legs looking gorgeous in her white shorts.

Now what do I do? I lay in bed and thought, worry streaming through my mind of all the "what ifs" in the world. I couldn't take her home. Anne was there.

"Let's go for brunch," I suggested. "Silverlake has dozens of great places for brunch. Mary's Place down the street is terrific. They've got a seafood crepe that will knock your socks off." She didn't have any on — sandals had appeared out of the satchel as well. "Or what about Chinatown for dim sum?"

A glance of wariness passed over her face. "Sounds good. I told you, I've got the whole weekend! We can do anything we want! Hey, what about Magic Mountain? Charles is an old stick-in-the-mud. He never wants to go on roller coasters. I've been dying to try out the big ones ever since I got to L.A." Expectantly she awaited my reaction.

I hate roller coasters. I even vomited over the

side of one, the green fluid spewing down a hundred feet onto bystanders below. Not one of my prouder moments.

"It'd take too long to get out to Valencia and back. I have to work tonight. Maybe the merry-go-round at the Santa Monica Pier?"

"Great! I'd love it!" She kept nuzzling me while I tried to put on the fresh clothes I always kept in the apartment, ever since a drunk I was trying to 86 got sick on me one night at the bar. They come in handy — sometimes I have to shower and change on muggy nights when I've been dancing a lot. Oh well, might as well admit that I'd made sure to bring over one of my best outfits, a steel-blue jumpsuit that matches my eyes.

We walked over to Mary's Place for the seafood crepes, marveling along the way at every pink daisy and flame salvia and blue bachelor button in people's front yards, ignoring graffiti and cracked sidewalks. Mary's Place was crowded with men. Good for me, I thought, that these men wouldn't be interested in the beautiful woman I was facing over breakfast. Fulfilling their own morning-after fantasies, the male couples wouldn't give us a glance.

I worried that my face showed morning puffiness, that my beginning crow's feet and sagging jawline would be off-putting in the sun. She looked even younger in sunlight, her skin a pale cream with her hated sandy freckles showing as plainly as a farm child's.

She kicked off her sandals and walked across a patch of lawn, giggling at the tickles underfoot. " 'Barefoot girl with cheeks of tan . . .' " I couldn't remember the rest of the poem. She put the shoes back on when the lawn ran out and broken glass took its place.

Santa Monica in fantasy is far nicer than the reality these days, and yet it still is one of the most wonderful cities I know, as long as you look in the right directions. Every big city has its areas where you don't look, where your eyes slide past the occupied cardboard crates, where you don't see the guy walking with that hesitant gait many junkies seem to develop. I'd stick to the wealthier streets. In Rhonda's convertible we drove in fits and starts through Sunset Boulevard traffic — there's no easily accessible freeway to the coast from Silverlake — and followed the Pacific Coast Highway to a cutoff that ducks under an overpass and into the pier's parking lot.

Too many of metro L.A.'s millions of residents had had the same idea, not unusual on a beautiful Saturday in June. We dodged hustlers and teenyboppers and toddlers and dog shit to get to the stairs to the pier, where the crowd was even more packed.

The wait for the carousel was a quarter hour. Rhonda leaned back against me and I ran my hands along her body, making a desperate attempt at discretion in this public place, wanting to tug the bandeau up and the shorts down, forcing myself to be content with the snug feel of her waistline, her body against mine, her hip rubbing against my pubis.

It was a disappointment to have to move when our turn came. We debated taking one horse, decided they were built for children and we shouldn't press our luck, and allowed ourselves to hold hands while riding a matched pair of striding palominos. The cool plaster soothed my groin.

No more excuses to snuggle close when the ride was over. We got in line for the ride again, using the opportunity to neck outrageously. Pat Parker would have approved — we couldn't have been more blatant.

"Aren't we going to get kicked out?" she asked, breathless, as we remounted our horses. We stuck with the palominos.

"You mean women don't do this in San Marino?" I laughed.

She shook her head and reached over and kissed me, then looked around in wonderment at the other riders and passersby. One old man glared at her. She turned red and looked at me.

I shrugged and said, "Ignore him," leaning over for her to kiss me again. With a mischievous glance back at the man, she did. We almost fell off our saddles.

"Want to do it again?" I asked.

"Let's walk in the ocean." She leaned against me as we made our way through the crowds down the stairs to the sand. We stopped at the car to dump shoes, wallet and purse in the trunk. We waded along the shore, dodging the highest waves that splashed our sun-warmed legs and our lust-warmed thighs.

I let my hand run under her bandeau and up her back, smoothing away imaginary tensions, recapturing the timing of our lovemaking. She leaned harder and harder against me until I lost my footing and landed on my rear in the water, pulling her down onto me. A crashing wave drowned out our laughter.

I fought to keep my head above water as she teasingly tried to dunk me. We kissed again, cold waves splashing through my clothes against my nipples and into my vulva.

We held close and kissed as wave after wave outside crescendoed into wave after wave inside, pulsating through our lips into each other and back again. I moaned and pulled away.

"I need you now," I groaned. Unable to think, I pulled her up and into deeper water. I found a level place where we could still stand up against the highest peaks and yet keep our bodies mostly hidden between waves.

We kissed, salt water making our mouths hungrier. Her clothes were unyielding, rolling up tightly in the water. I held her up with my left hand while my right went for her vagina and her clitoris inside those clinging shorts. She held on for dear life with one hand, while the other undid the bottom buttons on my jumpsuit and delved into the hot places that cried for her.

I could see her nipples through her bandeau and fought the need to take them in my mouth. My mouth stayed on hers while our hands replayed the patterns of the night before.

We clung together as one, trembling. In turn, we each came with heat counteracting the cold Pacific. A wave larger than any of the others knocked us off our feet while we were still in the throes of tremors, and we fought to regain air. For a second I lost touch, and I could see a strand of hair floating on the surface; I grabbed it and yanked her head up above water.

"I can swim, I can swim." She laughed, spitting out water and rubbing her face and eyes.

"That's a relief. I was worried I'd lose you." I hadn't had time to really think what it would have been like if she hadn't come up. I wasn't going to think about it. No need now.

Holding her tightly, panting, I dared to look around. No one was paying any attention. Only in Los Angeles. And maybe San Francisco, Key West, Provincetown . . .

Gradually we cooled down and I suddenly felt ridiculous standing waist-deep in the ocean, fully clothed, struggling to keep afoot through the tide, having just made love in broad daylight in front of hundreds of thousands of people, even if they didn't seem to notice. Someone might have; any second a lifeguard might arrive and place us both under arrest for obscene behavior in a public place or some such law. "We'd better go," I said.

I took her hand and we stumbled ashore, avoiding the faces of the people we passed in case any had been watching. I especially avoided the lifeguard in his tower. Did we give him a good show? I didn't even want to know if he had binoculars.

"We were pretty stupid," I said. "We could have been arrested."

"Why? We didn't do anything wrong. Nobody had to look if they didn't want to." She was brazen, still flushed with loving.

"Yeah? What if two straight teenagers were making love on the beach in plain view. Or two gay men. Wouldn't you have been offended?"

"Probably."

"Would it be wrong for them?" I tried to corner her.

"Maybe not. Not if they cared for each other as much as we do." She glanced shyly over at me.

I felt the "L" word in my throat, the other "L" word, even if I knew better than to say it aloud this soon.

"I care for you, too," I let myself say.

We reached her car. She had a towel and an old *L.A. Times* in her trunk, which we put over the car's tan leather seats and sat on until we dried out. The wet newspaper felt rank and heavy underneath. Our clothes were clogged with salt. We left off our shoes, Rhonda breaking another law against driving barefoot.

We dried quickly as we drove, arriving back at the parking lot of Samms'. My four-year-old blue pickup was there, alongside Tim's Saab. I got out of the car and pulled the wet newspaper off my skin. You could read the headlines on my legs about a drive-by gang shooting. I rubbed my skin until the headlines disappeared into black sweaty balls.

She got out of the car and helped pick away the inky paper blobs, giving me an extra stroke between my legs. She was ticklish and giggly as I returned the favor. I forced on my shoes to protect against the slivers of glass gleaming on the asphalt parking lot.

"Now what do we do?" she asked, holding me tight and leaning against me in the bougainvillea-covered rear garden entrance to the bar. The tiny clear Christmas tree lights strung throughout the bushes and shrubs twinkled in the sunlight even with no power surging through the green wires.

"I don't know, what do you want to do?"

"I want to see where you live. I'm starved, and I think I'm in the mood for cooking you a good, hot meal. Please?" she begged.

Anne could be home. Even if she wasn't, signs of her would be all over the house.

I tried to think of alternatives, of ways to stall Rhonda, of ways to tell her the truth. Any second, and it would be too late.

It was too late.

Her eyes clouded over and her jaw clenched. "You can't take me to where you live," she said in wonderment.

"Why . . ." She slumped. "You still live with that veterinarian! Tell me the truth, it's not over between you. Tell me!"

I couldn't open my mouth.

She straightened again, fury showing on her face. She was pouting like the babydyke she was.

"Goodbye, Silly Samms. Give me a call when you make up your mind." She grabbed her purse and rushed back to her car, knocking her shin against a garbage can.

Muttering under her breath, she heaved open the door and slammed it shut behind her. She flattened the accelerator and roared out onto Hyperion like a drag racer.

"That's right, go home to your fucking husband!" I yelled, too late for her to hear.

I couldn't move. Against the side of the pickup I collapsed, finally opening the door to hide inside the car. Stunned, I pummeled myself into the car seat and tried to let the feelings out.

The sobs stayed inside and plugged up my sinuses and gave me a retching headache. I collapsed, unable to think, unable to even plan a way to explain. Under the pain was anger — at Rhonda for being a silly little kid, acting like an adolescent telling off a boy during recess, and at myself for expecting more out of a babydyke.

My elbow hit the car horn. I tried to cover my face as Tim came to the rear door to check. Then he saw me. Wet, filthy, with a pallor of dried salt channeled by tears, I must have been some sight. I tried to wipe my face and look like the boss. I wasn't succeeding.

Tim took one look, saw from my expression that if he took one step closer I might hit him, or at least fire him, and went back inside.

Being alone in the parking lot was a relief. Then it hit me: I was really alone.

I might never leave the truck again. Once I could see straight I might drive to the desert and never stop. I thought aimlessly of Alaska, or Mexico. Of Kahlua, vodka and milk. Of hell.

CHAPTER SEVEN

Reality set in. I couldn't stay in this tiny cab forever, however much I wanted to. Dried salt water cracked on my hot, sweaty skin. My clothes were heavy with it. My joints creaked when I opened the door and slid onto the asphalt. I tried to tiptoe inside and into the back room before Tim or anyone could spot me. It didn't work.

"Hi, the day's been quiet so far. Need any help?" Tim's cheery voice boomed across the bar, his eyes darting behind me for signs of Rhonda.

"You can stop looking for her. She's not here."

My head reeled. "I'm going to take a shower and change, and then I'll take over and you can go on home. I'll pay you for the rest of the afternoon anyway. Check back tonight around nine and see if we need you."

No, I couldn't give up this easily. "I've changed my mind. I'm glad you're here, Tim. Why don't you just carry on? I don't know when I'll be back, but Carmen's due at six. Nothing's coming up you can't handle."

I left him and retreated to the apartment. All the clothes I had left after the shampoo and shower were last night's slacks and a Silly Samms' Sluggers T-shirt. No way could I face seeing Anne at home today for something nicer; the outfit would have to do.

Tim discreetly ignored my leaving, though I could sense his interest, his desire to make a judgment or offer "help" in a way that would allow him to control the situation. Was Anne right, that every man, no matter how nice, feels he has the right to advise women what to do and to judge their behavior?

I know I'm a strong woman, and yet I'm still uncomfortable around men sometimes, even very sweet gay men who don't seem to have a sexist, racist thought. I had other problems right now than mentally debating Anne.

Back in the hot cab, I had second thoughts. Sure, Rhonda had said that her husband was out of town for the weekend. But what if there were church people at her house? I could call but she'd probably hang up on me. And what could I tell her anyway? Should I rehearse something to say, and risk sounding like a phony, or did I trust myself to wing it and risk sounding like a fool? I almost turned the S-10 around.

San Marino, like Bel Air, always intimidated me. The mansions give off an air of isolation and superiority. Sure, the very rich put on their designer jeans one leg at a time, but they want that distance, they need it, to protect themselves from intrusions. Like me.

I drove to the English Tudor parsonage. No other cars besides the yellow Mercedes were parked in the drive, so I felt safe going to the door. The knocker was a wrought iron lion's head; I grabbed it by the nose and slammed its mouth shut to make a thunking sound.

As I waited, I wished I'd risked seeing Anne and gone home to find another shirt. Sweat soaked my T-shirt, droplets trickling between my breasts, chilling my nipples despite the heat. Or was that fear?

Rhonda's footsteps clipped lightly on what turned out to be a marble floor. The heavy hardwood door swung open. I caught it when she tried to slam it shut.

"Rhonda, you let me make love to you. You at least owe me the courtesy of hearing me out. You're not a one-night stand." I grimaced as we fought over the door. I won. There are benefits to size.

Her rounded figure slumped, like an antelope shot by a tranquilizing dart not quite strong enough to make her drop. She had on a short pink floral terry robe and shower thongs, her damp hair in a high ponytail. Her eyes wouldn't meet mine. I tried to reach out for her but she resisted.

"I'm not going." I was inside the door now and it

had to be clear she couldn't force me out. If nothing else I outweighed her.

"All right. Let's go to the kitchen." She led the way down a dark oak corridor to a room that must have been twenty by thirty feet, also oak-paneled. We sat in the breakfast nook, the bench seat padded with brown leather.

"Do you want coffee?" She looked wary and drained.

"Only if it's already made." She poured from a Braun coffeemaker into stoneware mugs and warmed them in the microwave, setting a matching stoneware sugar bowl and milk pitcher in front of me. She took hers black.

She finally sat down and seemed to will her eyes to meet mine, reluctant though they were. "So what do you want?" Her pained expression taunted me.

I'd decided to wing it. Wrong choice. Now what should I say? Maybe that I didn't know what to say.

"I'm sorry you ran out on me this morning," I began. "Anne and I broke up. We haven't been lovers for more than a year, and I made a deliberate point of breaking up before you'd even said one word to me. You weren't the reason we broke up. We've had problems for years. It was over a long time ago."

As best I could, I went through my life history once more, this time in more detail, though I still noticed I was de-emphasizing Anne's role.

"Lesbians don't always lead motherhood-and-apple-pie lives," I explained. "Some of us have forged whole new ways of living, of relating to each other. We don't have the rules already set up for us like straight people. We're deliberately kept out of those legal systems." I gave her my example of the Moslem man who can divorce his wife by saying three times, "I divorce thee," and how I'd wished I had a more definite, clear-cut breakup with Anne, akin to a legal divorce. "I don't have a piece of paper to show you, but we're not together anymore, even if we still live in the same house."

"You said she knows all about me. Then why couldn't you bring me to your home?" Her eyes were accusatory.

"Yes, she knows about you, but it would be like rubbing salt in a wound to show up with you. I know it's hard to understand . . ." Looking into her eyes was like looking down into a frozen lake through the snow. "But a lot of lesbians have different kinds of living arrangements. Anne and I bought that house back when prices were low. Neither of us could afford a house alone. Well, maybe she could, but I'd be back in an overpriced apartment."

I shook off the thought of what life ahead might be like away from the house. I love that place. But the end was near. *Don't think about it.*

"The house is big enough for two separate lives," I continued. "Maybe we will sell the house one day. Maybe she'll want to do that soon. Her lawyer and accountant are figuring out the best way to split the assets. But it's a great house, with a big front porch, on a hill overlooking Silverlake, at the end of a cul-de-sac, all wooded, and I like living there."

I gulped the coffee. "We bought the bar together, too, and if we sell the house she might want to sell the bar, and I can't afford to buy it from her outright. I don't know what kind of terms she'll come up with. I'm hanging in the wind. Look, this makes it sound like all my arrangements are made around money, and I guess that's kind of true. I never had money like this." I glanced around the *Architectural Digest* kitchen.

"I never had money before, either," Rhonda interjected, obviously irritated at the implications of that glance. I was making a mess of it.

"I'm sorry, Rhonda. I know you don't care about money that you didn't earn. I didn't mean it the way it sounded. I never was much good at most jobs, and I can't imagine myself tending bar for somebody else. I'm spoiled. I've had a pretty good life for the past twenty years, I have to admit it. But, something big has been missing. And then I met you." I dared to meet her eyes. Her face softened.

As I told her more about the house, and the pets, and the garden, and the view, and about how Anne's son lived with us and how he had come to accept us, Rhonda's face changed. I didn't notice it right away, but when I stopped to sip my coffee, I saw that she was no longer with me. The distance between us had grown again, though we were still just a few feet apart across the butcher-block tabletop.

"You still love her," Rhonda stated simply.

"No, I don't," I protested. "We're still good friends, and that's to be expected. We've got a history together. I expect we'll always be good friends. I didn't stop liking her. I just stopped loving her."

Rhonda made a sad, tight smile, almost a scowl. "Laney, I believe you believe that. But I can see you do still love her. You're a family. And that's okay, I don't feel so used anymore, now that I know the whole story. You don't want to admit to yourself that you still love Anne, for whatever reason. But I can see it in the way you talk about her, about your life together. You're totally dependent on her. You're both totally entwined —"

"That's just the money —"

"And not just the money. You still love Anne. You should be trying to work it out with her. It doesn't sound hopeless to me. Besides, it's much, much too soon for you to be with another woman."

I was frozen in place.

She relented, and reached out to touch my arm. "It's okay, I can see that you're trying to do the right thing. But it's just not our time now. I had a wonderful time last night and this morning, probably the most wonderful day of my life. You're a terrific lover, and I'm grateful."

I tried to interrupt her again — *grateful,* for God's sake — but she silenced me.

"Okay, grateful is not a good word. But you said yourself that lesbians trying to . . . come out, you said, are often seeking that first sex experience just to see how it is, to see if they really are lesbians. So I was, we did, and I am. A lesbian," she said, almost proudly. "I really am a lesbian. I never felt that way with a guy. So I don't know what comes next. I guess I'll just have to leave my husband soon . . ."

A tear ran down her cheek and made a dark spot on the butcher block. She was quiet for a minute. I saw how her hair was starting to dry into wispy curls around the edges of her ponytail.

She spoke again. "Do you know I just realized my hypocrisy here?"

For a second I couldn't follow. I was too heavily in grief for what I'd almost had. Then I heard her, heard myself mutter in response, "About time."

"I deserved that," she admitted, jutting out that tiny pointed chin that set off her otherwise round face. "I'm still married, none too eager to leave this comfortable house, and I have the nerve to be angry at you for living with someone else and not immediately leaving your comfortable house." She looked genuinely shocked and sheepish.

So she hadn't heard my last yell to her earlier this morning as she was leaving the bar parking lot.

"I guess I just don't feel married, I don't think I ever did. You and Anne have . . . something special. Something Charles and I never had."

This time she let me take her into my arms. I slid onto the bench next to her and held her while she cried and clung to me.

"Oh Laney, I've missed so much. I want to have love so much. I don't know what I'm going to do." She was sobbing again.

I stroked her red-gold waves and kissed her forehead. I wanted her more than I have ever wanted anything in my life. "Maybe if we take time, take it slow," I whispered.

She sat up and pushed me away. "No, you and Anne belong together. But I want desperately to be your friend. I need you to . . ."

". . . help you find your way around as a lesbian," I completed her sentence.

I wasn't happy with the role, but it was better than being cut off entirely. Maybe at some point she'd see that it was Rhonda and I who belonged together. I decided not to voice that thought, in case she thought I was scheming again. Not me.

"Look, Laney, I'm going to come around to your bar again, if that's all right, but I'm going to be looking for someone else. Someone who's really free." She brushed aside my renewed protestations. "Is that all right?"

She looked at me with round eyes that were definitely green against the red swollen lids. She had on no makeup. I wanted to kiss each freckle.

Instead I kissed her once, lightly, on the lips, forcing myself to hold back. "It's all right, Rhonda. I'll help you any way you want. But don't expect me to introduce you to prospective lovers to replace me — I just want you around so I can be with you. Just so you know where I stand." And bide my time until the right moment to make my move again, I added to myself.

"I appreciate your honesty," she said simply. "Honesty is important to me."

I felt like a creep. We were both hypocrites. "Friends we are, then," I said.

"Friends," she said, and reached up to kiss me on the nose.

I felt like James Dean in *Rebel Without a Cause,* trying to win Natalie Wood away from her boyfriend when she kissed the boyfriend on the nose and chin. Just before he drove off a cliff.

I felt as if I were hanging precariously on the edge of a cliff myself. Would I win, or would Charles? Or someone else entirely?

Natalie-Rhonda was edging me toward the front door. Before she opened it to public view, she kissed me one more time. “I’ll be by the bar again tonight,” she promised. “But I warn you, I’m going to try to meet other women.”

“That’s okay,” I lied.

CHAPTER EIGHT

Rhonda showed up around nine, wearing the tight jeans and a scoop-neck, sleeveless aqua T-shirt. Her red-gold hair hung long and loose, curling over the side of her face like Veronica Lake's. She wouldn't know who Veronica Lake was.

Making her way through the crowd to a solitary empty seat at the other end of the bar, she just waved and then motioned to Carmen.

Carmen looked over at me and I shrugged. Rhonda gave Carmen her drink order, though my bartender kept glancing at me. I deliberately kept up a conversation at my end of the bar while the white wine was delivered. Carmen wasn't the only one looking at me.

As soon as she could slip away, Carmen worked her way over to me. "She dump you already?" she asked.

Despite the bluntness, there was a genuine concern. I appreciated it. I'd definitely have to make her manager if I kept the bar. "Thanks. Yeah, it just didn't work out." Was my hurt showing? I shrugged again.

"Ah. Okay, well, all right then." And Carmen gave me that disgraceful broad wink as she left. I really needed to speak to her about that.

A crowd of friends down at the other end soon discovered Rhonda — at least one of the women did — and brought her into their conversation. She was asking questions of each one, I could tell, and they buzzed like drones around a newly emerged queen bee. I was jealous and turned away.

I tried to bury myself in a raging pseudo-political argument over whether there were more Muslims, Buddhists, Protestants or Catholics in the world and what that portended for the end of homophobia. Bad choice. Better we had been arguing over batting scores. When someone suggested calling the nearest Catholic church to have a priest give us some statistics and settle the argument, I bowed out and washed glasses.

Next thing I knew, Rhonda was dancing with a woman I vaguely recognized. Rhonda never looked at me. I couldn't stand it.

Carmen was at my side again. "Fast worker, that

one." She jerked her head toward the dance floor. I ignored her.

"Who's that woman she's dancing with?" I finally asked when desperation got the better of me.

"Her name's Lydia Munoz. She just left her husband a few months ago. She's got two little kids."

"They live with her?" Suddenly I knew why Rhonda had picked Lydia out of that crowd of friends, and what she had been asking them.

"No, the father got 'em."

"What's he do? Stay home with them?" I wanted this Lydia's life history, and Carmen seemed to sense it. Besides, this was her forte, running a communications network from her outpost at Samms'.

"All I know is it's a good job, and his mother takes care of them during the day. Lydia couldn't afford them."

"What's she do?"

"She clerks down at that big discount house on Echo Park Boulevard. She's got a tiny place in Echo Park and she wants to go back to school. She felt bad about it, but she couldn't keep the kids."

I didn't blame her.

"The bastard probably would have fought her for them anyway, and brought up in court she was gay. A Latina can't risk that," Carmen said knowingly.

"Most Anglo women can't either," I commented.

I looked hard at Lydia. She was maybe twenty-three, with jeans as tight as Rhonda's, a white cotton shirt that buttoned on the right, black cowboy boots tooled in a red scroll design. Shining black hair as long as Rhonda's, swinging straight and thick. They looked good together. I turned away.

"Get back to work, Carmen," I ordered.

"Yessah, boss, right away, boss," she mocked me over her shoulder. I disappeared into the apartment and tried to do some bookkeeping.

The night was interminably long. I emerged from my cave a little after one to see Rhonda leaving with Lydia. An immense headache ran from the back of my neck all the way over the top to my eye sockets. "I'm going home. I'm sick," I told Carmen.

"Hey, Tim never came back. He called to say he worked this afternoon instead. And Nancy's dragging her tail tonight. I need help."

"Oh, right. Tim worked the day. I need to stay." First I found the Tylenol, then I started shoving out the drinks, one glass at a time. Keep on living responsibly, one day at a time. Clean and sober. The smell of beer nauseated me. But if anyone ordered a white Russian I was in trouble. No one did. Thank you, HP.

"She wasn't worth much anyway, that one," Carmen tried to reassure me. Carmen was in all black, her signature color. Somewhere she'd read that you can never go wrong in black, and her prayers on dealing with fickle L.A. fashions were answered. It would have worked in New York.

"What do you know about what she's worth?" I snapped.

"Hey, just trying to cheer you up, Silly Samms. Huh, should be Stupid Samms, far as I can see." She winked.

"Unfortunately, you got that right. And quit that

winking. You look like some leering macho prick." That wasn't quite how I'd meant to bring up the subject. She looked shocked. "I'm sorry. I just have a horrible headache."

"You got that right," Carmen mimicked me, disappearing as I snapped a dish towel in her direction.

The week crawled along. Anne showed up at the bar Friday night with Cheeka, her new vet tech. They seemed to have a good time. Again, I had the feeling everyone in the bar was watching me for my reaction. I had none. I was a robot behind the bar, watching my formerly beloved Anne dance cheek to cheek with someone named Cheeka. I wondered if it was the Latina equivalent of Bambi or Candi.

About twenty-five, Cheeka had short black hair even curlier than Anne's. Her slim hips, packed into white pants, gyrated seductively to a Gloria Estefan tune. What was it with old geezers and younger women, I wondered. This Cheeka should be with Lydia and leave Anne alone. So Rhonda would be left alone, it went without saying.

Why should it matter to me, I asked myself. I'd taken a chance and lost. I couldn't have it both ways.

Why not, the immature kid inside me whined.

Higher power, deliver me from myself, I prayed. Why couldn't I just say "Lord," or "God," instead of this higher power shit? But I couldn't. The AA "Big Book" is too deeply ingrained in me, word for word. The phrases rolled in my head.

HP, it's you and me against the world. I am helpless against alcohol without you. I have wronged myself and others. I have tried to make amends and turned my life over to you. I want my shortcomings removed. I want to carry what I have learned to others and to practice my newfound principles in all my affairs.

It sounded empty, phony. My HP was out to lunch. I sighed. Maybe I needed a meeting. It had been years; maybe that was my trouble. I should have stayed tied in, showed up at a couple meetings a month to testify that yes, it can be done, addiction can be licked, look at me, nearly twenty years sober. Nineteen years passed one day at a time. Cheeka left with Anne and I called the 24-hour AA hotline to find out where there was a group meeting scheduled for Saturday morning.

I had to drive to an old church in Venice to find one. The leader was a wanna-be Burt Reynolds looking for his Loni, a thirteen-stepper if I ever saw one. I let him know immediately I wasn't the one. My first sponsor had warned me about guys who think AA is just a sober singles bar, adding their own agenda to the twelve-step program.

But I testified about my history, my twenty years' sobriety, and how tenuous it all felt right now. I was in trouble, all right. I couldn't plug in.

A few hugs helped, but not enough. Some good advice, parroted right from the Big Book but still valid, the latest literature, and tight hand-clasping during the closing prayer gave me a boost. Wanna-be Burt offered to be my sponsor, get me back on track. I declined and wiped that meeting off my list.

When I got home, I called Tim to open for me and spent an hour with my dusty copy of the Big Book before Anne walked in for lunch.

"Hey, long time no see," she said.

"Just last night."

"I mean just you and me, here. Sometimes I get the feeling you're dodging me. How are you?"

"Fine." I wasn't about to tell Anne my troubles.

"Things are fine with me, too." She opened a can of water-packed tuna. "Want some?"

Anne puts chopped green onions, celery and sometimes water chestnuts, walnuts or pimentos in her tuna salad; I just stir in mayonnaise.

"If there's any left, thanks." I felt uncomfortable taking the sandwich on thick wheat bread from Anne. It was delicious.

Her hair was growing out. Trying to look younger to keep up with Cheeka? No way was I going to ask that. At least she hadn't dyed it.

I'd briefly thought about finding a blondish shade to cover the pure white which I'd had since my twenties. It was a great conversation piece when my face hadn't matched it. But I couldn't quite bring myself to do more than think about it. Laney, Priscilla, Elaine, Silver, Sil, Silly, Stupid. Laney Samms, a real piece of work.

Now Anne, there was a woman who'd kept her integrity, even while having a fling or whatever she was doing with the kid. Even in hospital greens, she looked alive, happy.

As if sensing my scrutiny, Anne looked directly at me and insisted on eye contact. "You're looking good, Laney."

"Thank you." Good for an old piece of shit. I didn't believe her, but I wasn't up to a confrontation. Maybe it was because I hadn't eaten lately. I devoured the sandwich.

"How is your new friend?"

I growled, "It didn't work out."

Anne stifled a smile. "Umm. So I heard." Then her face turned serious. "Are you okay about it?"

"Yeah."

She stood up, put her plate in the dishwasher, covered the bowl of tuna salad with foil and put it in the fridge, then wiped her placemat.

I would have never thought of those things — I was the one who left food out until it spoiled, who forgot to wash a tablecloth for dinner parties, who never noticed the spider webs in the bathroom. I glanced around the kitchen — she'd been doing heavy-duty cleaning, I could tell.

A chill crept over me. Maybe she'd been cleaning up for Cheeka. In my house. No, our house, and not really that. I wished fervently that I was rich, that I had enough money to extricate myself from this mess, that I didn't have my nose rubbed in my mistake every time I went home.

"Cheeka and I are going to see Lily Tomlin tonight at the Schubert — want to come along?" Anne asked. "I know where to get another ticket, if you can get off work."

"No, the bar's been pretty busy lately. I'd better

be there. Thanks, though." No way would I be a pathetic third wheel. I rested my face in my hands.

Anne touched my shoulder. "I'm sorry," she said. When I dared lift my face, the tears firmly in abeyance, she was gone.

Rhonda showed up at nine that night, alone. She approached me, and I could feel my chest grow tight.

"Hi, I came a little early — Lydia's coming at ten," she said, as if I were all right with that. I wasn't. "I need to talk to you." She looked at me expectantly. I didn't know why. "Can we go in the back office?"

I refused to bring Rhonda back to that room to talk about her and another woman. "I'm pretty busy. Can't we talk about it here?"

"Oh, of course. Well, I guess so." She took a deep breath. She was taller. I looked down at her very high-heeled black sandals, to go with her black pleated slacks and sleeveless lacy blouse. Lydia must be influencing her to dress more femme.

Stop it, Laney, I told myself.

"I wonder . . . have you ever had to deal with a jealous husband?" she began. "I mean, he came home last Sunday and he asked what I'd done all weekend. That's the first time he's ever asked me anything. I'm worried."

"What did you tell him?"

"The truth, sort of. I said I went out with some girlfriends and we'd stopped off for a drink."

"How'd he react?"

"He took it okay. I guess. I just worry, that's all. Do men . . . ever get violent over this?"

"Men get violent over anything — some men anyway. You know him better than I do."

"I guess so. I just wondered — how nasty do these things get?"

"Extremely nasty — read Roxanne Pulitzer's book about her divorce, and she wasn't really even a lesbian, though that's what the Pulitzer family testified in court."

"I wonder . . ." Rhonda looked downcast, not what I would expect from someone in the throes of a new love affair.

I had to ask: "Are you sleeping with Lydia?"

"It's none of your business," she said instinctively. "No, I guess it might be. I did ask your help. The answer is no, not yet. We've been talking on the phone all week. I might go over to her place tonight."

I didn't want to hear all this. She kept on, each new bit of information a stab in my chest. "Last week we went out for breakfast at two a.m. I thought it was kind of silly, but it seemed to be the thing to do." Her eyes questioned me.

"Yeah, I can't do breakfast before nine a.m. myself." May you both choke on your eggs tomorrow morning, I wished silently.

"Is it all right to order something else besides breakfast?"

As if I cared? I continued this farcical conversation. "Sure. There are no rules for 'proper lesbian behavior' on dates. Don't straight people have breakfast after going to a bar, too?"

She looked embarrassed. "I guess so. I just sense that something else is going on sometimes. I think there's a lot more to this lifestyle than appears on the surface."

"You got that right," I said, immediately wondering if I was overusing this phrase, and how many times did I use it in a day? From now on I'd count.

"Well . . ." She was still hesitant, apparently with more to say. "I guess that's it. I guess I just have to wait and see what happens."

"Takes time," I glibly assured her.

She looked as if she were going to reach up and kiss me on the nose again. I couldn't have stood it if she did, so I busied myself with cleaning out an ashtray.

" 'Bye, Laney," she said.

She and Lydia left when the bar closed, the last couple out the door. I couldn't stand to see them kissing. Rhonda pulled her yellow Mercedes out of the well-lit parking lot and followed Lydia's Honda down Hyperion. I couldn't help watching the cars travel out of sight. I sighed and went back inside to make out the deposit. Maybe I would spend the night here. Depressed as I was, I didn't want to risk seeing Anne.

It was three-thirty a.m. when the phone rang at the bar. Surprised, I assumed it was a wrong number, or a drunk, but I answered anyway.

"Oh Laney, I'm so glad you're still there. I was going to call your house but I worried about getting

Anne." It was Rhonda. "I went to Lydia's apartment and she never showed up! Have you ever heard of such a thing?"

"What happened? Last I saw, you were following her home."

"She gave me the address to her place when we were at the bar, in case I lost her — I told her I'm no good at following people. I saw a 7-Eleven on the way and stopped to buy some stuff for breakfast, in case I wanted to cook something."

Rhonda didn't seem to think this happy little scenario would have any effect on me. She kept on babbling. "When I got to her apartment there was no sign of her. I waited out on the street but it felt dangerous to be in a convertible at night. She doesn't live in a very good neighborhood."

That didn't surprise me. Divorced women rarely do. Perhaps Rhonda would, with all that money.

"Could she have stood me up? Do women really do things like that?"

"People do things like that," I answered slowly. "I don't know Lydia very well. Look, maybe she had a flat tire. Maybe *she* stopped for groceries at the all-night Mayfair. Don't assume the worst." Don't call me for advice on your love life, I wanted to add.

She was crying on the other end of the line. "She should have said. I waited more than half an hour on that terrible street, and men kept driving by and looking at me. I got scared. I drove around some and then I drove by again and her car still wasn't there and so I left. Maybe it isn't worth it. I was happy before . . . I was."

"If you say so."

"Women aren't any nicer than men," she said

between assorted crying sounds. "I didn't expect that."

"Yes, we are . . ." I started to say. But then I said nothing. Stupid babydyke, living in fantasyland. I couldn't bring myself to hang up. I hung on, silently. At one point I thought I heard two breaths when there should have been one. And was that a faint click?

Breaking through her sobs, I asked, "Where are you?"

"At home. That's what I should have done, don't you think? I couldn't wait out there all night."

"Where's your husband?"

"Oh, he's sleeping. He must have finished taping his sermon early tonight. I peeked in, he's sound asleep."

"He can't listen in on an extension, can he? Do you have a phone in your bedroom?" Their shared bedroom, I noted grimly.

"I told you, he's fast asleep. I just checked."

"Better go make sure. Maybe you need to be more careful. Maybe you should see a lawyer now. Maybe he'll do things like tape your conversations and use them against you in court."

"Don't be ridiculous, Laney. Charles would never do such a thing. Anyway, I called you about Lydia, not about him."

"You know him better than I do. Good night, Rhonda." I debated saying I was sorry. I wasn't, so I didn't.

"Good night, Laney. I'm sorry I bothered you. I'm glad you were still at the bar. I needed to talk to someone, and you're . . ."

"The only one who would understand. Yes, I

know. Good night, Rhonda. Sleep tight." I waited for her to hang up, then looked at the Kahlua and vodka. Time to get out of there fast.

I called the 24-hour hotline from home. There was a Sunday morning meeting in West Hollywood.

CHAPTER NINE

It happened too late for the Sunday *Times,* but I heard about it at the bar that afternoon. Lydia Munoz had been the victim of a drive-by gang shooting. She was dead on arrival at County General.

Her white Honda was found crashed into the hillside of a section of Riverside Drive where it parallels the freeway, a tall brick sound-wall on one side of the street, a sheer cliff rising on the other. I'd once thought, driving that stretch, that it would be a lousy place to have a flat tire.

The police were looking for witnesses, but it wasn't likely that anyone would have been on that section of road at two-thirty Sunday morning.

Except the gang members who must have been shooting at each other from passing cars when Lydia's Honda drove in the wrong place at the wrong time. That's what the police were theorizing, anyway.

I debated calling Rhonda — to tell her she hadn't been stood up, it was much worse — but I didn't want to antagonize her jealous husband. She'd have to hear it sometime, but the story might never hit the news.

Lydia wasn't exactly a prominent person, and one more drive-by shooting wasn't exactly headline material. L.A.'s crime was so bad that most murders never even made it to the news. "Only the juiciest," a woman with the D.A.'s office had told me when she wandered into the bar one night seeking a moment out of the closet.

All summer we'd had a crush of drive-by gang shootings. Maybe Lydia would be a name in a story tallying the weekend's violence, or maybe not at all.

She was a paragraph in Monday's paper, page seven.

It wasn't until Monday afternoon at the bar that I got the call from Rhonda. She was hysterical. "Laney, I have to see you." Her voice choked on the other end of the line.

"You heard."

"Yeah, on the radio, just this minute. I'm so upset. I just need to talk to you."

Mentally I reviewed the employee schedule. Mondays are generally slow, so I usually handle the day myself. I could try to reach Carmen, Nancy or Tim. Or close the bar. Only one lone drinker was nursing a beer.

I didn't have to plan. Rhonda continued, her voice choppy, "I'll come there. Right now. Will you be there?"

"Of course. See you in half an hour or so?"

Slamming down the receiver, she didn't say goodbye. I pictured her dashing from the house, her husband staring at her retreating back.

She must have done sixty through the downtown streets. At the sight of her coming through the door, I told my boozy customer that she'd had enough to drink, I had a family emergency and needed to close the bar for a short time, and her tab was on the house. Under protest, she left.

I put out the "Closed" sign and steered Rhonda into the back apartment and sat her down on the sofabed, which I hadn't closed since she'd been there. I comforted her and stroked her hair while she collected herself.

"Things like this didn't happen in Horseshoe. That's the town where I grew up. Horseshoe, that's right. Stupid name. Things like this don't happen in San Marino, either."

"Welcome to Los Angeles," I murmured.

She didn't notice. "Lydia was so full of life, I can't believe she's gone. It was so senseless. She was so young."

I'd gotten hardened to young people dying the past few years. I kept silent while Rhonda sagged against the pillow.

"She was just in the wrong place at the wrong time, that's all," she murmured to herself.

I could sense tension in her, the kind that built along her backbone and extended into her flexed feet and clenched hands. She nuzzled my neck. She kept on settling in closer to my body, tugging me back onto the bed. I didn't know what to think.

She stopped, waited, apparently thinking. Or agonizing. "Laney, this is a terrible thing. I don't know why I'm even saying it. You're going to think I'm a terrible person. But I want you."

She held me tighter and began rubbing her hands up and down my back. Hard. I could feel the heat rising. But it wasn't right.

"You're supposed to be here being comforted on the death of the woman you were about to fall in love with. You were going to sleep with Lydia just a couple days ago."

"I know," she answered, and didn't stop.

She was relentless. I wasn't sure I wanted to, wasn't sure whether I was being forced to do something I didn't want to do. But of course she wasn't forcing me. Nobody was saying no. I could have left at any time. I didn't.

She became more and more frenzied, stopping short every so often as if she didn't know what to do next, didn't know what she was doing. She pushed up my T-shirt and sucked hard on my breasts, to the point where I did have to push her away. At least from there. She thrust her hands under my waistband, not waiting until I felt ready. She'd made up my mind for me, for us.

Her fingers were awkward but insistent. I found myself sliding out of my pants at her unspoken demand. The T-shirt came off next.

So strong, so fast, so demanding. No way could I stop her. Or myself.

We were on dangerous turf again, just as we had been at Santa Monica Pier. No gentle, mutually acquiescent lovemaking of the sort that seemed to be the "politically correct" lesbian goal. I'd even heard lesbians argue that passion was impossible between true equals, between those who maintained egalitarian relationships. Bullshit.

Women get mad when they hear — usually from men — that they really want to be forced, that they fantasize about tough, demanding, forceful sex. Maybe it's because a lot of men think we want it that way all the time, from anyone. But I'd sometimes fantasized about letting go, giving up responsibility, being taken — by someone I wanted to take me. I'd thought about this before, when Anne and I had made comfortable love, quiet sex that might even prove correct the theorists who say equal lovers can't let go and rut like rhinos. Can't or shouldn't — we're supposed to be above all that, maybe because men seem to have claimed that territory. Anne had made me feel like I was betraying her feminist sensibilities when I tried to let go, to get her to let go. But ravishing lust had been my unspoken fantasy. I'd never gotten it in real life, not before now.

Was this experience Erica Jong's zipless fuck, lesbian-style? At least it was Rhonda's style, my style, right at this moment. Maybe never again.

I absolutely could not help it. I responded to Rhonda's touches, her tongue, her fingers, with a furious orgasm that plummeted me deep into the mattress and bounced me high and plummeted me deep again.

Of course I could help it. I willed her to go on. I willed my letting go. Which philosopher claimed faith was a blind leap over a bottomless chasm? So is love. I leapt.

Rhonda hung on, whimpering, groaning, growling, and pushed me down against the bed once more and forced me to come over and over again.

I was letting her give me my orgasms. Did that mean I'd lost control? Could I stop her if I wanted to? Did taking away all desire to stop her mean she'd won the ultimate victory? And was it a victory for both of us, or just for her? Was this merely a different kind of control than Anne exerted?

Rhonda said my name. At least she said "Silver," my name when I am a hot-blooded dyke stud, a name I had long ago cast off. Silver it was. I was glad she at least knew who she was with. For intense seconds when I was careening off walls in my agony/ecstasy, I didn't know who she was, who I was, where I was.

"Silver," she wailed again.

"Rhonda," I echoed. An earthy, sexual name, sounds which pulled at my innards, pulled something out of my guts that I didn't know was there. Rhonda.

Never had I had sex like that. I wondered if it would ever be possible again. Who cared? To have it once in a lifetime might be enough.

And yet . . . I kept feeling pushed, like someone was trying to push me off the bed itself. The word *rape* formed in my head and I pushed it away. I hadn't pushed her away. Maybe I should have.

Forty-eight years of *shoulds* rolled over me like an avalanche of ice crystals, chilling me to the bone. It was wrong to feel this deeply. Wrong to whom? The ice crystals smothered me like a shroud of diamonds.

It was over. At least for me. Out of the corner of my eye I knew I had a duty now, to give back what I had just been given. I wanted to make it all right, to slow down, to put some love into our lovemaking.

That was not what she wanted.

Her hips thrashed, demanding that I pleasure her. She tugged me onto her, arms flailing, her elbow accidentally catching me on the temple, my knee hitting against her pelvic bone with a strength that would leave a bruise on her hip by morning. Not a safe thing for a married lady. She grabbed my wrist in a vice-like grip and shoved my hand between her legs like a quarterback snapping a football. I felt helpless and gave her what she needed, moving faster than her past rhythms, harder than she had previously liked, pushing hard to the point where I was afraid I would leave scratches inside her.

She didn't care — if she had bled she wouldn't have cared, I was sure. She pushed against my head, forcing my head against her until I could barely breathe, making my tongue plunge deeper and harder and faster. Her juices poured into my mouth and down my chin and onto the sweaty sheets.

I slid all over her mons, catching the clit when I could, fingers sliding deep inside her pulsing passage. Her hands worked her own nipples, her teeth bit her lip, her eyelids clenched tightly together. A faint pattern of freckles appeared all over her breasts and chest. Sweat poured in rivulets, trapped in her curls, her cleavage, her navel, her groin.

She came with a shriek that would have caused the customers outside to call 911 if anyone had still been there. The scream turned into a wail.

More sobs. She pushed my face against her mons till I couldn't breathe, till I felt I was drowning in her. I heard growls, panting, wordless sounds that I knew would forever echo at the edges of my dreams. And perhaps my nightmares.

"I shouldn't have done this," she said, sitting bolt upright and searching for her clothes. I didn't know what to help her look for; I hadn't noticed what she'd worn, only that it had come off effortlessly. A rolled-up wad on the floor turned into white shorts, the same ones she'd worn when we'd made love in the ocean; a lime-green sleeveless sweater untangled from the sheets; tennis shoes appeared when the rug was yanked away. She retrieved them soundlessly, dressing in haste. In a moment she would be gone.

I was suddenly afraid I would never see her again.

"This was really wrong," she said as she left, speaking more to herself than to me, slipping the latch off and leaving me in a naked heap on the bed. Stunned, unable to move.

I knew then that I would never see her again. I pulled a wet sheet over me to stop the sudden chill.

An eternity later I got up and dressed and

walked in a daze into the darkened bar. I sat down at a rickety wood table and traced a heart someone had carved in the table.

"Cheryl *con* Nikki," it said inside the heart. "Forever."

I got up and made myself a white Russian and gulped it down. It slid into place as if it belonged there, searing away the pain. All the rough edges smoothed out. This was right. Why had I fought it?

Then I made another. There was no milk for the third.

When the Kahlua was gone I drank the vodka straight. When I felt wobbly on the barstool I let myself slide down to the floor and sit there with the bottle until the liquid wouldn't go down anymore. I couldn't lift the bottle to get the last sip out. The bottle was heavy. So heavy . . .

I heard noises of crashing bottles and felt myself being moved around, and I thought, I should be scared, I should check on what's going on, I should open my eyes. They wouldn't open. My head hurt. The blackness slid over me again like an eclipse totaling the moon. I swam out of the blackness but couldn't find the light. My eyes were glued shut. Something was moving me around. I should wake up. Why couldn't I open my eyes? Something wet was dripping in my mouth. Or out of my mouth. Vodka. I'd thought the bottle was empty. One more sip to stop the pain.

I slurped on the liquid pooling by my mouth and

gagged. It was warm. The vodka had gotten warm and thick and it didn't taste too good. It needed Kahlua and milk . . .

I felt arms grabbing at me again, or still, throwing me around like a rag doll. Silence for eternity. Now voices, lights, sirens. I should open my eyes. They still wouldn't open. I worked on lifting one eyelid with all the tenacity of a marathon runner up against the wall of pain around the twentieth mile. Keep working that muscle. I shifted the attack to the other eyelid. When it finally relented, the shaft of light pierced like glass.

Carmen's face swam into view, shrieking. I winked at her. I watched a needle prick my arm and wondered why I didn't feel it. Maybe I'd never feel anything again. I was being bounced around and men were holding me down. I tried to break away and couldn't, so I went back to sleep. Such a comforting sleep. Sleep for eternity.

CHAPTER TEN

I must have turned into a spider: my multifaceted eye picked up dozens of versions of the same face, that of a male in a white coat, peering down at me. The face made sounds I didn't understand. Kafka was almost right. I closed my eyes — they still worked, the glue must have worn off.

When next I could open them, my eyes saw a new sight: different faces in each facet. How could that be? Gradually I realized that a dozen new faces surrounded me, scrutinizing me. Maybe they were the spiders. Some of the faces were black, brown, gold, white; some had beards, some had glasses. Only one talked, a small face with thick black bangs covering her eyebrows. She said words like *acute alcohol toxemia* and *miracle* and *two-point-eight* and *past the danger point* and *concussion* and *possible fracture.* When the faces disappeared I slept again.

"You can only stay a few minutes." A saccharine voice floated into my ear.

"Is she conscious?" I recognized that voice. It was Anne. Where was I?

"Laney? Are you awake? Her eyes are open!" Anne's voice flooded me with relief. She was here, she forgave me, she'd take good care of me. From somewhere careened the thought that I didn't need to be taken care of. Oh yes, I did, shot an answering volley that destroyed the struggle for independence. At least for now.

"That's wonderful," said Saccharine. "I'll put it on her chart. Remember, just a few minutes."

Anne was crying, her salt-and-pepper curls all mashed together like tangled hemp. "Laney, you're alive."

Had that been in question? I had another: "Where am I?" The words hurt coming out. What was in my mouth? My tongue couldn't force the rubber thing out.

"The emergency room at Hollywood Prez."

"What happened?" Then I remembered. I tried to turn my head away and ran into a nasty tube down my nose that hurt when I moved. I looked away from Anne instead, spotting what must be a mirror of myself in this bed but instead was another woman in another bed. Beyond her was another occupied bed, and another. My eyes must be doing the multifacet number again. I deserved to be Kafka's cockroach. "I drank." I could say nothing more.

"Your blood alcohol level was almost to the fatal level when Carmen came to work Tuesday and found you. Luckily you passed out. Your body didn't have any tolerance after all those years. You hit your head pretty bad, too."

I couldn't respond. There was nothing more to say.

Saccharine came and took Anne away. "I'll be back later," Anne's voice was saying. Why would she bother?

A white-coated man I first thought was George Bush put on a thin smile when he turned to me after skimming my chart. He turned out to be a psychiatrist, and each of his visits were exactly five minutes — he looked at his watch while I kept an eye on the wall clock behind the nursing station. He told me I was depressed and needed to think positive thoughts about starting over. I'd been given a second chance. I'd been given a new clean slate. Yeah, sure, squeaky clean. I pondered ordering him out of my room — rather, the oft-invaded footage surrounding my bed that I still felt was *my* space —

but decided I'd get out quicker by playing along. Though the bed did feel safer than whatever awaited me in Silverlake.

I was surprised, when I remembered more, that Anne came to see me several times. After the first yellow-and-green pill made me sleep twenty-two hours straight, I got Anne to use her medical authority to convince the psychiatrist to take the antidepressant off my regime. He said he'd find another that I could tolerate better, but then I never saw him again. Guess one of those faces decided I felt better. I didn't, but the pill hadn't helped.

Anne called my old sponsor from AA, who drove in from Long Beach to see me and get me plugged into a schedule of meetings, ninety meetings in ninety days, more if possible.

Carmen, Nancy and Tim all came to see me and vowed to keep the bar running so smoothly that no one would miss me. They'd made all the plans for our float in the Gay Pride Parade, which as usual would simply feature the bar's softball team, waving and flirting with all the dykes along the parade route, and of course no one expected me to ride with them this year.

Max showed up with a bouquet of daisies she'd picked from a neighbor's yard; I barely heard her gravelly voice through the potent sleeping pill they'd given me, though I never wanted to sleep again after the antidepressant. Anne tentatively renewed the issue of selling the bar and said her lawyer and tax consultant were at work on ways to separate our finances. All of this went in one ear and out the other while my body recuperated.

* * * * *

I was home in the waterbed with a cup of what Anne called Boston tea — mostly warm milk and sugar with a tea bag dunked in it — on what used to be my bedside table. She let me use her comfortable bed for a few days while she slept on the sofa. Cats and dogs were all around me in lumps. Radar was sitting at my side, whining. No one else was home. There was a note from Anne that she would come home for lunch and I should call her if I needed anything.

I began the long process of recovering.

My first AA meeting as a newcomer was quite a comedown. "Hi, I'm Laney, and I'm an alcoholic."

"Hi, Laney." The response was routine.

"I've been sober for four days."

Cheers and applause. More than I used to get when I said nineteen years.

Burt Reynolds wanna-be was at my next meeting. He avoided me. I met two nice dykes from Culver City who took me out for clam chowder at the Red Lobster afterward. At least I could still laugh, though it made my facial muscles hurt.

Rhonda came by to see me at the house one Saturday night, when Anne had just fixed me a cup of Red Zinger tea and propped me up with pillows on the couch. She answered the doorbell and beat Rhonda into the family room. "Mrs. Preacher's here," she said coldly. "I'll leave you two alone." She disappeared into the kitchen.

Rhonda stood stiffly in front of me. "I heard you were robbed and got beat up pretty bad. I'm sorry." Her hair in a tight bun on top of her head, she wore a pale yellow shirtdress and flats. She looked like an old-fashioned schoolmarm.

"No robbery. Nothing taken. I got drunk, fell off my stool and hurt myself. People are saying I was robbed?"

"I called the bar to talk to you and Carmen told me you'd been beat up in a robbery."

"Well, maybe I was. Nobody'll tell me nothin'," I joked. I'd rather she not know the truth anyway. I couldn't remember if I'd mentioned my alcoholism in our truth-sharing. She probably could have guessed from my Diet Pepsi habit. At the moment, I didn't really care.

As I remembered how we'd had sex the last time we were together, I did not have any good feelings for her. I was thinking more of how Anne was feeling, alone in the kitchen.

Rhonda scrutinized my face. "You look awful."

"Thanks a lot." It still hurt to laugh.

The silence was even more painful.

"I guess I should go. I just wanted to come by and see how you are and tell you I'm sorry."

"Message delivered," I said, hoping no emotion showed.

"Laney, I've decided . . . I'm staying with my

husband. There's too much . . . too much involved in being a lesbian. I'm better off where I am. It's not so bad." The look in her eyes begged me to believe her.

"Bully for you." I was almost ashamed to cut her off so crudely. But it was worth it to see her recoil.

She left without saying any more. Her presence lingered, as if I'd faced down an intruder. How dare she come to our house!

I waited for Anne to come back into the room. She never did. I got up to check on her, and as I passed by the front living room window, a cracking sound stopped me in my tracks. I dropped to the floor, the quick move causing pain in every limb. I waited, breathless.

"Anne?" I yelled. "Are you all right?"

She came running and saw me on the floor. "Did you fall again? Are you okay?"

"Get down!" I sputtered. "I think there was a gunshot. Stay away from the window."

She dropped to her hands and knees and crept to the window. She dared a quick glance over the window sill.

"I see a car driving away, a black old one," she said. "It's a big monster, like one of those old Chevys. I can't see a license plate."

"Don't try." I reached up for the light switch to put us in darkness. When there was no other sound I crawled to the phone and dialed nine-one-one. "I'm on hold!" I announced, shocked.

"I don't believe it!" Anne got up and threw a sofa

pillow in front of the window, then another. "Don't laugh, I saw this on TV, it's to draw the fire of anybody still out there."

"I'm not laughing. Hello?" The dispatcher had finally answered. I told her the story and listened intently, ready to take whatever action was needed until the police could arrive.

"Two or three *hours?* Thank *you too,* Officer," I snarled and hung up.

"What'd they say?" Anne was examining the bullet hole in the window and looking in the dark for a matching hole in the living room wall.

"That a random bullet with no injuries is a low-priority call, especially on a Saturday night, and an officer would come by when one was available, but it might be two or three hours!"

She was as stunned as I was. We stood around in the dark for three hours before giving up and going to bed, checking all doors and windows before we did.

At three a.m. a sharp rap on the door and a voice announcing "Police," amplified by a bullhorn, brought us from our rooms back into the living room. We flung open the door to find two pistols aimed at our midsections. Our hands jerked up in the air.

"For God's sake, don't shoot us, we're the ones who called!" They holstered their revolvers. I restrained Radar from attacking the team of officers—a Latina who looked too young to be a cop and a heavily mustached African-American.

"So what's the story here?" the man asked. We told them. The officers looked at each other.

"Look, ladies," the man said. "We've got a serial

murderer hitting prostitutes on Sunset, there's a satanic cult sacrificing purebred dogs and who knows what else on Aaron" — he glared at Radar's bared fangs — "a couple dozen rapists and wife beaters have been reported tonight, burglar alarms are going off all over Rampart Division, the black and Latino gangs have gotten together to fight off the Vietnamese and Samoan gangs — you get the picture. Nobody was hurt, nothing was taken, your insurance will cover replacing the window, you didn't see anything except some 'big black Chevy,' and you have no enemies that are likely to be taking potshots at you, am I right?"

Anne and I looked at each other and nodded.

"So get some sleep. You find the bullet?" he asked the Latina, who had been giving our walls a once-over behind us. "No? If you do, keep it as a souvenir of Rampart Division. Good night, ladies, we've got *real* work to do."

Enraged, I sputtered, "Let me get your names, I'm going to report this."

"Whatcha gonna report, ladies, hmmm?" The officer shoved his badge in my face. I read it aloud while Anne scurried for a pencil. By the time she found one they were gone.

"What *would* we report?" Anne asked.

"Nothing, I just wanted to get at him somehow. That's twice we've been lucky — what else is going to happen? I guess we go back to bed." Radar and I retreated to our room and neither of us slept much; I was sure the same thing was going on in Anne's room.

Maybe we should sell the house, I thought as I lay in the single bed, Radar crunched up on my feet so I couldn't move. L.A. used to be a great place to live. Now you're not even safe in your own house from stray bullets. Like poor Lydia. Ever since the advent of crack, the gangs have been out of control. I fell asleep while making up tentative budgets, wondering how much we might get for the house, and what the attorneys might propose as fair. What else could I do for a living, though? Groom dogs again?

In the morning Anne found the bullet imbedded in the kitchen wall behind the stove and dug it out with a steak knife.

"It's pretty beat up," she said, tossing it into our junk drawer with the yellow plastic corn-on-the-cob holders, ceramic goose napkin rings, and steel shish kebab skewers.

In the aftermath of the incident, Anne and I didn't even talk about Rhonda's visit.

A few weeks later I visited the bar. Whether I'd been angrier at the person who shot into my house or at the cops, I was over it and feeling pretty solid. Carmen promised to stay alongside me the whole time I worked, and to not let me be alone for a minute, no matter what I ordered her to do. "Yessah, boss," I snarled at her. She winked.

In August the bar got its usual boost in attendance from the annual Sunset Junction Street Fair, followed by the annual summer slump. Few customers were in the bar the night Rhonda returned. It was September 8, two days before my forty-ninth birthday, though she didn't know that and I didn't tell her. Carmen, Nancy and Tim protected me by not letting her get anywhere near me, but she did manage to veer in my direction on her way to the bathroom.

Before Carmen or anyone else could get there, Rhonda told me, "I found out I couldn't take it at home. I am a lesbian, Laney. You taught me that." Carmen grabbed her hard enough to cause her to shriek. "Sorry, boss," Carmen told me, escorting Rhonda away.

The bar hosted a small party for me with a lavender-frosted sheetcake and a few generic candles. Anne didn't attend, though she sent a nice card. Also generic.

In the following weeks, Rhonda came in every Saturday night and sometimes on other evenings. Too quickly she hooked up with a very sweet thirty-something woman. I could almost approve, as long as I ignored our past. The woman's name was Karen, Carmen informed me, and she worked in the circulation department of a publishing house that specialized in automotive magazines. She was divorced and lived in Hollywood. Her teenage daughter had chosen to be with the ex-husband, who lived in a sprawling ranch in Palos Verdes with the new wife and a combined family income of $142,000 a year, compared to Karen's salary of $275 a week. The husband wanted child support from Karen.

Karen was a no-shine kind of person — dull brown, straight hair, blotchy skin, pale gray eyes, expressionless broad mouth, average figure, boring clothes. She was the kind of woman I almost wished Oprah would pick off the street for a make-over. I wondered what she had looked like before — had the divorce drained her? But Rhonda seemed to like her, and they met once a week at Samms' for white wine and low-key conversation — no raised voices ever came from their table, and neither danced to "I'm Bad." It seemed like an ordinary kind of relationship — ordinary considering that Rhonda was married.

Husband still hadn't said anything, and seemed resigned to her long absences. She was going to leave him soon, she said, the one day I dared to talk to her, having just left an extra-supportive meeting. After the holidays she'd bring up the subject with him. It was inevitable, she was just scared to do it. She felt good about the decision, and good about a new life with Karen. Good, I said. Life went on.

The holidays have always been tough for me. Having an alcoholic father meant that I never knew what to expect when I got home from school, and his various wives and girlfriends were just as unpredictable. While other kids looked forward to Thanksgiving and Christmas, I never knew what to expect. Would my father be on a "good father" binge and smother me with inappropriate presents like negligees or babydolls, or would the month go uncelebrated? Would the latest wife stick with him and put something together that would pass as a holiday celebration, or would he blot out the month with Smirnoff?

In therapy with Anne, I had discovered that as an adult I sometimes tried to recreate that exciting if devastating environment. With Anne I'd found a way out of that constant search for excitement, and after my recent adventures I tried to capture that secure life we'd once had, even though this time it was as roommates. Boring is better, that was my new motto. I wanted as little mention of holiday spirit as possible.

Anne had sent nice letters of resignation on behalf of both of us to our various organizations and backed out of all projects and promises. I had nothing left inside to give.

Cheeka seemed to be out of Anne's life, scared off by my experience and Anne's response to it, I supposed. She'd even quit her job, leaving Anne to find another tech. Anne didn't give me any of the details.

Rumors about our resignations and our relationship must have been rampant in the community, but I deliberately ignored the occasional probing question. Let them talk, let them imagine the worst. I went to work, I came home, I went to meetings, I went to bed, and I read the Big Book and the new AA materials and listened to tapes.

I even went through the twelve steps again, including the personal inventory of all the people I had wronged in my life, and forced a minister with Metropolitan Community Church to hear me read it aloud and grant me a kind of absolution. I began to feel okay with my life again. It was boring, ordinary, routine, but comfortable and safe.

I earned my ninety-day cake for attending the ninety meetings in sobriety and ate chocolate cheesecake with my new friends. One woman even flirted with me. My sponsor took her aside and said I shouldn't be in any relationship until I had at least a year's sobriety under my belt. She avoided me after that. I was grateful to my sponsor.

I dyed my hair honey blonde, then cut it off butch-short and let it grow back in silver again. In a West Hollywood men's boutique I bought a steel-gray leather bomber jacket that looked great on me.

I discovered three-dimensional jigsaw puzzles and had one going at all times at the bar. Anyone who had a free moment was welcome to paw through the two thousand pieces.

Radar came with me to the bar often. She sat tied up on the patio and developed a fan club. On the way home in the pickup, she leaned tight up against me. She slept with me every night on the twin bed. I learned to sleep without turning over.

At Los Angeles Community College I took a course in stained glass. Anne suggested it, on the basis of a remark I'd once made. I really took to the glass-cutting and the sour smells of flux and patina and hot solder. I loved the way I could maneuver the oiled glass cutter around a curve. It was like cornering a sports car — the snap was satisfying when it cracked right. Even the small burns around my wrists from the sputtering solder felt good.

I whipped through the easy projects and tackled a too-advanced stained glass window for the dining room. I was so proud when I took it home; Tim came by and helped us put it up. It could raise the selling price of the house a couple thousand dollars, Anne said.

Her clinic was going smoothly. She had a new assistant who was working out well, and her clientele kept building by word of mouth. She had no problems, while I, on the other hand ... My insecurities tried to drag me down. Easy does it, I told myself, one day at a time ...

We kept talking about selling the house and/or the bar, and where each of us might choose to live instead, but we never did decide anything definite. Then again, not to decide is to decide.

CHAPTER ELEVEN

On a Tuesday in mid-November, Rhonda's yellow Mercedes, with the top up, was waiting in Samms' parking lot when I drove up a few minutes before opening. I walked over.

"Hello," I said. She rolled down her window.

Her face was a mass of bruises. Dried blood caked along newly formed scabs. Swollen eyelids made it hard for her to look at me. Her red-gold hair hung lank.

"My God, what happened?"

"He hit me," she said, tears welling in her eyes.

"Oh, baby." I reached into the car to hold her.

"Ouch, it hurts too much."

"Sorry." I backed myself out of the window and just stood there, helpless. My insides churned.

"I don't want to go to the police," she said. "I don't know what to do."

"Tell me how it happened."

"Charles just started hitting me this morning when he tried to kiss me goodbye and I didn't respond the way he wanted. I get so tired pretending all the time. He started slapping me and pushing me up against the wall, and my head hit a mirror on the wall and I got cut all over from the broken glass. Then all of a sudden he came to and stopped, and he apologized and left, like it was all over and I should forget it ever happened."

I didn't know what to say. She looked so stoic, so determined. But she winced when she touched her cheek.

"Do you think he knows about Karen?" I asked.

"I'm sure he doesn't. How could he? I'm careful. He has to sense I don't love him. Guess that's enough."

"You could see an attorney, get a restraining order."

She thought a minute. "I've been wondering about that. I don't want to make a scene and get him any bad publicity. I owe him that much, to do this quietly. I guess I'm going to have to leave him. That's all there is to it. It's time. Only . . . I'm scared."

"He doesn't deserve to have you protect his privacy."

She gave one vehement head shake, followed

immediately by a small moan and tensed shoulders. "You don't understand, Laney."

She was right, I didn't. I wanted to kill the guy. Blast his face on the six o'clock news. He deserved it, the fucking hypocrite.

I still couldn't touch her, she hurt so badly.

"See an attorney," I urged her again. "He can't do this to you." I wished I were the one with the bruises instead of her. All my past resentments of her had vanished the moment I saw her bruised face.

"Maybe I'll talk to our family attorney. He'll be able to keep things quiet."

"Maybe you should find your own attorney, someone who won't side with your husband."

She thought about it. "I just want this kept quiet. I'll see what he says first."

"Promise me that if you don't get the feeling he's on your side, you'll find someone else?"

"Okay." She started to smile but grimaced instead. She turned her ignition key.

I backed off as she drove away. "Be careful," I said. "You don't have to put up with that."

"I will," she said.

"Good luck," I said to the departing car.

I went inside and cussed out husbands, and men in general, until Tim came in. My employees were still keeping an eye on me at work. It made me feel like a baby, but then that's what I was, not even half a year sober.

For my meeting that night I searched out a women-only group in Pasadena. I needed that support only women can give each other — hell, if some prick made any kind of stupid comment in a mixed group I was likely to punch him out, so I'd better avoid any men.

The leader was nearly sixty, sober ten years and still coming to three meetings a week. That had been my downfall, I realized, pulling out as if I were cured. Once an alcoholic, always an alcoholic, she reminded me. After the Lord's Prayer — our leader started it, "Our Father and Mother in heaven" — I let her hug me and hold me and rock me in my turmoil. I really was a baby. She smelled of rose oil.

On my way home I drove past the English Tudor parsonage but couldn't see a thing. The lights were on all over the house, a waste of energy, and their glow made the house look like a warm, happy, all-American home. I wanted to bust in and smash Charles's face the way he'd done to Rhonda. "Sure, that would solve everything," I admonished myself.

A few days later, the Friday night before Thanksgiving, Rhonda and Karen came into the bar around six, happy as kids playing in the snow. That's what they were going to do, spend the weekend hiking in the snow at the Rasmussen cabin at the far northeastern corner of L.A. county, north of Mt. Wilson observatory.

I took Rhonda aside and asked her if she'd seen an attorney. Her makeup was back again, so thick I could see nothing of her own complexion. This was Cindy Crawford's Cover Girl complexion, not hers.

"The attorney said he'd handle it. He'd get a restraining order, but he'd have to do it his own way to get a judge who'd keep it quiet. Charles should get the papers served on him sometime next week."

"Isn't it kind of risky, going away this weekend?"

"Karen and I have had this planned for weeks. Charles is at a conference. He already left this morning and won't be back until late Saturday. We'll beat him back and he'll never know a thing."

"I hope so, for your sake." I was concerned about this little outing they were taking. My expression must have said so.

"Don't worry about me. I'm going to have fun for a change," Rhonda said, jutting her chin, then wincing. I asked, "Does Karen know he hit you?"

"I didn't tell her. The marks are almost gone. I said I'd banged my face on a rake while I was gardening. Why concern her?"

"But it's okay to worry me."

"You're stronger than she is."

Was she crazy? Didn't she remember my little escapade? That's how strong I was. I opened my mouth to say something but she'd slipped back to Karen, linking arms with her, in a way that said clearly, one more time, for as many times as it took me to get it, that we were through.

Karen was still bubbling on and on about the trip into the San Gabriel Mountains.

I thought it was all federal parkland in that area, but Karen explained that the cabin was in a private hunting club preserve near where Highway 39 met Highway 2, by Throop Peak and the Kratka Ridge Ski Area. She knew it was going to be absolutely beautiful up there — clean air, lots of stars, no gunshots or police helicopters. I was jealous.

Where was the Rev? Off at a retreat for Episcopalian priests, to recharge their batteries for the holiday services, Karen continued to explain. And wouldn't you know it, the delicious part was that the retreat was at the conference center at Crystal Lake, only forty or so miles down the mountain drive from the cabin! Wasn't that ironic!

Wasn't that insane, I thought. I looked at Rhonda. She ignored me. I was totally baffled.

They'd have to stay out of the party shops and restaurants in case they'd run into him, Karen said — that was apparently the full extent of their plan to avoid him. Karen had a Jeep that they'd loaded with supplies, far more than they could possibly need, even firewood for the cabin's fireplace. I wondered when she'd stop for a breath as she prattled on to me, face to face as if we were lifelong buddies.

Rhonda went off to the john or someplace while this recitation was going on and returned to beam benevolently at Karen. Rhonda seemed proud to be able to put together this wonderful experience for this poverty-stricken, emotionally bereft, addle-headed, no-class dyke. Was my resentment showing? Anne wasn't around to see it, count my blessings.

The happy couple left in a flurry of last-minute best wishes and goodbyes from everyone else in the bar. I called my sponsor and had a long chat about bubbleheads and how to deal with them. And about long-buried anger and how to deal with it. And about sticking my nose in where it wasn't wanted.

I vowed to take it easy all weekend and try not to think about snow and fireplaces. And slap-happy husbands.

* * * * *

The phone rang at home and I heard Anne answer it in her room. The digital readout on my clock radio said seven-fourteen; I'd had four hours of sleep. I rolled over, dislodging Radar, pulling the light blanket over my eyes.

"Laney? Wake up, it's your Mrs. Preacher, and she says she's in trouble. She wants you to call her a lawyer." Anne's face in my doorway looked puzzled and annoyed.

"What's the problem?"

"How should I know?" She shrugged, handing me the phone. "Watch yourself. You know she's trouble."

"Rhonda? What's the problem?"

"Oh God, Laney, there's been a terrible accident. Charles came in on Karen and me and killed Karen, and I killed him. I need a lawyer bad."

"Whoa." She was talking so fast I could barely understand her. In total shock I pulled myself out of bed. "Start over. What happened?"

"Oh Laney, I'm only allowed a few minutes on the phone to get a lawyer and I don't know any. Not any that can handle this. Our family attorney is a joke — you were right. I need you to find me the best criminal lawyer you can find. Somebody with some experience in this kind of thing. It was self-defense, it was! But all this other stuff's going to be dragged in, and I don't know . . ." There were sounds of crying. Male voices barked orders in the background.

"Rhonda, where are you?"

"They're taking me to Sybil Brand Institute. Do you know where that is?"

"I'll find out. Don't say anything to anybody until I find you a lawyer."

"I won't. Laney?"

"Yeah?"

"I have to go. Can you come to Sybil Brand? I need to see somebody bad."

"I don't know what I . . . I'll find out. Don't worry."

"You have to come, Laney. I need you."

"Don't worry. I'll get there. And I'll find you a real good lawyer. We'll straighten everything out."

"Please, please help me," Rhonda sobbed. "Do I have to?" she argued with a man in the background. "Laney, I have to go. I need you. I —" Her voice was cut off by a click.

I stood up, shocked.

"What's that all about," Anne asked.

"She's being taken to Sybil Brand. Her husband killed Karen and Rhonda killed Charles."

"*What?*"

"I think she said Charles came in on them at the cabin. I don't know anything more about it than that. She got dragged away from the phone. She needs a lawyer, bad."

"Is this for real?"

I couldn't believe it. "Anne, she was calling from a jail someplace." I paused to take it all in myself. "So do you know any good lawyers?" I forced a thin smile.

"You're really going to get involved in this thing?"

"Anne, I don't have any choice. She doesn't have anybody. Who'll help her? Charles's family? Karen's?"

"There has to be somebody else. Why you?"

"Because I'm all she's got."

"I didn't think she had you."

"She doesn't! But she's in trouble, Anne. She

needs help, and I'm the only one who can help her! Are you with me here or not?"

"No, I'm not with you. You shouldn't get involved in this, not where you're at now. That Mrs. Preacher is a manipulative bitch. I don't trust her — neither should you."

She was right, I didn't feel any too stable, but what could I do? I told Anne that.

"It's your funeral," she said, turning to leave.

"Anne, at least give me some names of lawyers."

"I don't know anybody like that, my lawyer's only good for financial stuff."

"Well, call her and see if she knows anybody. Come on, Anne, at least do that much."

Her lawyer wasn't in at that hour, but the answering service, once convinced it was a real emergency, tracked her down at a Bar conference in Santa Barbara. She came up with two names, both criminal law specialists in gay- and lesbian-related cases. One was available.

It was a he, Randolph Greene, and he could meet Rhonda at Sybil Brand that morning. I got directions to the place and found out how and when I could visit.

The murder was page one in the Sunday *Times,* after Channel 2 broke the story Saturday afternoon. Noted Episcopalian priest, Dr. Charles Harold Rasmussen, from a prominent Bucks County family, related to the Wilson Rasmussens of San Marino who owned a chemical company in City of Commerce, was killed shortly after midnight

Saturday morning by his wife, Rhonda, after he found her with another woman reputed to be his wife's lesbian lover. Dr. Rasmussen allegedly shot the woman, a Mrs. Karen Sanders, who was divorced from Joel Sanders, prominent Palos Verdes business owner of a Baskin-Robbins franchise in Torrance. Mrs. Sanders was the mother of a thirteen-year-old who lived with her father and stepmother at the Palos Verdes home. Dr. Rasmussen's father was the owner of Rasmussen Transport, whose trucks and trains moved ore and coal from mines throughout Pennsylvania and the East Coast. Mrs. Rhonda Rasmussen was being held on a quarter-million dollars' bail at Sybil Brand Institute. Despite the family's wealth, she was unable to come up with the twenty-five thousand dollars required to meet the bail immediately, and her lawyer was attempting to unfreeze the couple's assets to raise the money. She was taken to Sybil Brand, the women-only jail with facilities to handle cases in which unusual security measures may be necessary, or in which unusual publicity may be generated. Mrs. Rasmussen's attorney was Randolph Greene of Century City, best known for his successful defense of Jeffrey Schoen, the self-admitted homosexual accused of murdering his AIDS-stricken lover who had repeatedly attempted suicide and failed. Greene claimed his client had shot her husband in self-defense, and he expected her to be released without a trial as soon as the investigation was complete. Dr. Rasmussen's parishioners at Christ the King Church in San Marino expressed shock at the death of their pastor . . .

When the story turned to quotes from these

parishioners, and from anyone else reporters could dig up on short notice, I stopped reading.

Streaked with blood, Rhonda looked wan in the photograph of her taken as she was being shoved into a police car at Crystal Lake. In a file photo, Dr. Rasmussen looked like a saint in his priestly robes, presiding at the wedding of another prominent couple a few weeks earlier. Karen's high school photograph was used. The cabin looked peaceful in the snow.

I went to three meetings over the weekend, not able to say anything about the murder. I didn't want to be mentioned in future stories. AA confidentiality is a joke.

It wasn't until Tuesday that I could comply with all of the red tape involved in visiting someone at Sybil Brand. I had to get there by 7:30 a.m. to wait in line to put in my name and my driver's license so they could run a check on me. Then I could come back in a couple of hours and wait in line again outside to hear if I'd be allowed in.

There'd be a minor search. I wouldn't have to worry about being strip-searched, or my body cavities invaded or anything. I couldn't even imagine such a thing — the thought hadn't entered my mind. Now all I could think of was Rhonda bent over, nude, some uniformed matron with rubber gloves sticking her fingers up Rhonda's vagina and rectum.

I'd have twenty minutes, and I could only see her through a glass partition. We'd have to use a telephone to talk. The lawyer called ahead of time to warn me that conversations might be recorded, so be careful what I said. Greene could come and go as he pleased; lawyers had free access to their clients in another area of the jail.

He also passed on some requests from Rhonda for toiletries and clothing. She could only have support pantyhose or white kneesocks, and two sets of plain white underwear, new, in their original packages. She also needed shampoo, toothpaste for sensitive teeth, toothbrush, tampons, deodorant and hand lotion. Everything had to be unopened, in original packages, with tamper-proof seals.

I drove to Glendale Galleria, remembering ruefully the last time I'd purchased underwear, and guessed at Rhonda's sizes. I had a heck of a time finding plain white kneesocks. Were they out to turn the prisoners into either old ladies in the support hose or kids in the kneesocks?

Tuesday morning I hit rush hour traffic all the way out to East L.A. via three freeways. Signs pointed the way to Sybil Brand and I pulled into the gravel parking lot at 7:27 a.m., along with hundreds of other people with the same idea. I'd been told only so many would be allowed in, and we didn't know how many were already inside, so we all speed-walked toward the check-in point.

I grabbed for a number from the guard. Sixty-three — I didn't know if that was good or bad. I was highly conscious of the barbed wire, the warning signs about following all regulations, the uniforms, the guns.

What a conglomeration of people here to see prisoners! I tried to keep my prejudices in check, but some scuzzy specimens could not have been up to any good. Just looking at them, I was sure whoever they were visiting was guilty, guilty of anything and everything. And then there were the families — the mothers, the kids, the grandparents — with sorrow in their eyes for however their female relative had gotten to this place.

For a moment I worried that somebody might see me and somehow associate me with these hopeless victims gone astray, that somehow it would rub off. I was guilty by association — I felt it, just as I'd judged that the women inside were guilty because of the looks of some of their visitors. Racism and looksism live, even inside me.

It was a gray morning, and the mist turned to drizzle. There were far too many people to fit under the pavilion roof adjoining the guards' station, even though we squeezed. I hovered on the edges, one shoulder in the rain, rotating every so often like a chicken on a barbecue spit, to distribute the wetness. A strong wind kicked up and spread the rain on everyone, even those lucky enough to be under the roof.

A guard shouted something unintelligible on a microphone. We snapped to attention. It was time to hand in our licenses and our bags of new underwear and to fill out the forms so we could be "checked out." I wondered if I had any outstanding parking tickets I'd forgotten about.

We pushed forward like lemmings, and the guards watched us, bemused, like parents watching toddlers at play. Or cats toying with mice.

"Sixty-three," said the voice on the microphone.

When I'd pushed to the front I gave my name obediently and filled out the white card. The guard grabbed it and my license from me and called out the next number. I stood there, not knowing what to do next. Someone told me to come back by noon, and maybe I'd get in around one. Maybe not. It was nine-forty. I remembered seeing a McDonald's right off the freeway. Maybe I'd hang out there.

Three other people in McDonald's were from the pavilion. We didn't admit to recognizing each other here, out in the real world. That had all been a bad dream — who, us, know somebody in jail? Not us, never been there.

Somebody had left most of an *L.A. Times,* minus the sports and want ads, the sections I'd least wanted to read anyway. I ignored the follow-up story on the murder. No, I had to read it. It was mostly a rehash, with more in-depth stories on the late rector's many accomplishments, heavy on his Harvard years. Rhonda's parents back in Pennsylvania were reluctant interviewees, saying that they had no idea how anything like this could have happened. Rhonda had been a well-behaved child, so promising. No, they hadn't had any contact with her in recent years. Funny, the paper said they lived in a small town called Backdraft. I was sure Rhonda had called the town Horseshoe.

One of her teachers at the Philadelphia nursing school said Rhonda was a bright and disciplined student, a caring human being, who would have made a wonderful nurse. No, she hadn't had any contact with her in recent years. Rhonda's neighbor said she had a lovely rose garden and was a good neighbor. No, she hadn't talked to Rhonda much.

The current director of the Gay and Lesbian Community Services Center, a lesbian, made some good comments about homophobia in our society and how many lesbians felt they had to hide their sexual orientation because of society's oppression, and how if society would just accept us, tragedies like this one would never have to happen.

I ate my french fries one at a time, prolonging each step of the eating process. Someplace I'd read that each McDonald's was designed to discourage long stays — the previous padded booths were replaced with hard seats some time ago. Though you could feel comfortable in the restaurant, you weren't likely to take up a seat too long. This encouraged high turnover and higher profits.

My attention started to wander. I tried to find something else to do. Nothing. There was a bar on the next block. I could spot it if I squinted. "Pistol Dawn," the neon sign said. Cute, but no thanks. When I couldn't stomach another bite, I drove back to the jail and leaned back against the S-lO's headrest.

I didn't dare nap in case I slept past noon; it was 11:02. The radio featured inane macho deejays doing stunts like calling an unsuspecting dupe and telling him his expensive sports car had been stolen. Yuk, yuk.

At noon a few car doors opened and in the misty rain a sort of ballet ensued, people pivoting and pirouetting and lifting small bodies that danced and twirled in the gravel.

Visitors were let in, a dozen families or so at a time, for their twenty minutes with a prisoner. My name was called at 1:35, and I underwent a superficial frisking by a woman guard and was given a slip of paper before being ushered through another chain steel gate.

I was in a courtyard facing three buildings and many doors, without the foggiest idea where to go. I stood there like a fool until the next woman pointed me toward one door.

We speed-walked together, excitement building in both of us as we neared the door and collided, both of us trying to get in it at once. "Sorry, after you," we both said, and collided again. How could we laugh at a time like this?

"I haven't seen Krista in three years," she confided in me. "Krista's my daughter. I was almost glad to get the call from her lawyer because I didn't know where she was." It had been three and a half days since Rhonda and Karen were at Samms'; that was a lifetime.

We were in a room about fifty feet square, with lots of corridors and doors like a rat maze. Another guard checked our slips. The other woman was told she'd have to wait and was ushered to a wall where a family of three hovered, waiting too. I was led to booth eight.

It was mass confusion, at least to me, as people came and went in no apparent pattern. The prisoners stood out, wearing ruffled pinafore jumpers or matronly polyester pantsuits in pink, yellow or blue, on the other side of the glass windows and steel walls.

It took a minute to recognize Rhonda, in one of the pink pinafores over a starched plain white campshirt. The uniform made her look much smaller. A rubber band kept her unwashed hair out of her face. Her pale legs were bare in plain white tennis shoes. Her freckles were distinct. She looked about thirteen.

Rhonda's blue eyes widened when another guard pointed to booth eight. "Laney, you came!" she shouted, running toward me. The glass barriers between us muffled her voice.

"Hush your mouth and don't run," the guard said. Rhonda slowed down obediently. She sat down in the metal chair on her side of the glass and picked up the phone.

The phone on my side was sticky with unidentified lumps. Oh well, I'd wash my hands afterward, I wrote up a mental Post-It note to myself. The glass too was smeared with greasy hand prints. I wondered if it was bulletproof.

In each of the adjacent booths, three or four people fought to share one phone to talk to their loved one in their allotted twenty minutes. I had Rhonda all to myself. I remembered that the phone might be bugged.

"Oh, Laney, you can't believe how glad I am to see you," Rhonda said. "It's horrible in here, just horrible."

"I can imagine." No, I couldn't. "Your bruises . . . did the police beat you?"

"Oh, that was from the other night, left over from Charles." Now I could see that they were yellows and greens, no longer blacks and blues. Rhonda shrugged. "The police haven't been too bad. It's the people in here, the guards . . ." She shivered and went on, "The attorney came. Thank you. I like him. He says I'll get out on self-defense, the prosecutor has no case."

"What happened? Oops, you probably shouldn't tell me anything on this phone."

She looked as if I'd committed a faux pas — apparently no one talked about the bugged phone while they were on the bugged phone. Let's all pretend it doesn't exist.

"I've got nothing to hide, I'll just tell you what I told the police when they came, and I told them again after Randy came and we talked."

Randy. Randolph Greene. "What's he like?" I asked.

"He's good. I trust him. We talked a long time and he told me to just tell the whole story to the cops. Just tell the truth, that's what he said, and that's what I did."

"You told him about the beating."

Her hand went to her faint bruises. "Yeah, and he's talking to our attorney. I mean the Rasmussens' attorney. You were right, the guy was strictly on Charles's side. He's probably telling the cops I did it to myself. But I think I'll get out soon. Don't you? If Charles wasn't a Rasmussen I'd be out already. Has there been any publicity? I hope not . . ." She had to know there would be.

Did she have to ask? "Do you get the papers in there?"

"I haven't seen any."

"Maybe your attorney should show them to you."

Rhonda went paler. "I hoped there wouldn't —"

"Look, forget about it. The papers say your lawyer thinks he can get you off without a trial. What happened?"

"Laney, you wouldn't believe how horrible it was. Karen was making popcorn and I was getting a fire started when there was a knock on the door. We weren't expecting anyone, I didn't want to answer it, but I thought it might be somebody with car trouble. Out in the middle of nowhere you can't ignore somebody in trouble."

I shrugged.

"So I opened the door and it was Charles! He pushed his way in and I ran and he shot at me and missed and I ran for the closet where he stores his birdgun and I heard a shot and he hit Karen and then he shot her again. I found the gun and he aimed at me and I shot him and he fell down. I ran to him and lay down next to him to see if he was alive and I couldn't stop crying and I lay there forever and I think I passed out, and finally I came to and realized where I was and what had happened. Laney, you can't imagine how he looked — the birdshot punched holes all over him, he was an unbelievable mess. I could barely tell it was him."

The family on my left was fighting over who got the phone next. I cupped my ear to hear better.

"I checked on Karen and she was dead. Somehow I'd known that before, from the way she looked, and I tried to find a pulse or something on Charles, and they were both dead. I didn't know what to do, there's no phone in the cabin, nobody in the other cabins, no place to call from. So I tried to clean the blood off my face at least and I ran down to the road and flagged down a motorist — it took forever for someone to come. The guy took one look at me and didn't want to stop. He wouldn't open his door or take me with him, but he rolled down his window a few inches and said he'd call the police from Crystal Lake. The cops said I was walking around in a daze when they came. I told them what happened and they still put me in handcuffs and put me in the back seat of the car and took me in. They read me my rights just like on television."

She took a breath, then continued her rapid-fire explanation. "I told everybody exactly what happened, but they didn't believe me. They couldn't understand the bruises. They kept trying to figure out how I got them in the fight at the cabin, and I kept trying to tell them there wasn't a fight, it was all over in a couple of seconds. I kept waiting and waiting in this little cell in the back of this little log cabin police station, while all these guys came and went and made phone calls and talked to themselves and I couldn't hear what they were saying and they were talking about me."

I had a lot of questions that I couldn't get in until this moment. "Why don't the police see it was self-defense? What are they doubting?"

"The problem is, he dropped the gun when I aimed at him, but it was too late. I couldn't stop, he would have killed me, I know it. But the police examined his gun and saw it had no birdshot marks on it, so they knew he'd dropped it before I shot him. They're trying to say he never meant to kill me, that I should have stopped myself from shooting. Somehow I was supposed to keep this monster at bay while I got the police somehow. There wasn't even a phone anywhere to call police. It *was* self-defense, Laney, he was going to kill me just like he killed Karen. Nobody believes me. You believe me, don't you? I told you how jealous he was. You saw how he beat me up first."

Vaguely I remembered her saying he was jealous when we first met. "I believe you, Rhonda."

"Thank you," she cried, reaching toward the glass. I put my hand against the window too. It may have been my imagination but I felt some warmth transfer through the partition.

She managed a wan smile. "Randy believes me, too. He says I won't be held, they're only keeping me because of who Charles is. Was. The investigators are at the cabin. They'll have to see what I said is true, that's how it happened. Oh, Laney, I'm so glad you came. You can't believe what it's like here."

That was still true.

"Why are some of you in pink and some in yellow and blue?" I asked. What an inane question — what did it matter?

It did. "Oh, that." She looked down at her pinafore ruefully. "We pinks are 'special.' We're either charged with murder or really serious crimes, or we're high publicity, or there's something else different about us. Did you see three older women in pink when you came in?"

"I have no idea. I didn't know what I was looking at."

"They're nuns, arrested for some protest against nuclear weapons someplace. I want to talk to them but I haven't been able to yet. We pinks are in our own cells. There's another pink around someplace, she's a porno star, they say she's behind a kid porn distribution ring, too. She doesn't look like it. Her name's Krista. She's real young."

"Umm, I think I met her mother."

"Oh yeah? What's she like? Listen to me, good grief. I don't care about her mother. To think I used to watch 'All My Children.' Now I'm living it. You wouldn't believe the stories I've heard."

I still didn't.

"If I stick around here any longer I'm going to be an old hand at crime." She tried to laugh. It choked in her throat and the tears poured out again. "Laney, I'm so sorry for what happened between us, I wish, I wish things had been different."

"So do I."

"You're the only person I have in the whole world, besides my attorney, and I hope I've got enough to pay him. My money situation is a mess. I don't know what's going to happen on that. I can't think about that now. I'll pay him somehow. I just gotta get out of here!"

"You will. Don't worry, everything's going to be all right," I said, not sure that was the truth. "It sounds like a clear case of self-defense to me, even if he did drop the gun. I don't know why you're being held at all."

"Charles's father and mother flew into town, Randy told me, and they're trying to quiet things down. They hate any negative publicity — you say Randy should be able to show me the papers? God, I hate to think what they're writing. Did the . . . gay thing come out?"

I nodded.

"Oh God, his parents must love that. I don't

know what they can do, but money talks. They want to see me fry."

A male voice boomed something through a microphone. "You have to go," Rhonda wailed. "Come back tomorrow?"

"I don't know if I can. You can't believe what I had to go through to get in here."

"Yes, I can," she said, twisting her ponytail around her finger and biting on the ends. "I have to leave — they don't mess around here. I'll see you as soon as you can get here again, Laney, and thank you again for coming. You don't know how much it means to me."

I thought maybe I did.

"Oh, did you bring the underwear and deodorant?" she asked as a matron came to take the phone from her hands. I mouthed "Yes." She looked relieved and made as if to smell her armpits —"I stink!" she mouthed back.

Laugh to keep from crying.

CHAPTER TWELVE

I walked slowly back to the parking lot, unable to comprehend the day. Poor Rhonda. The attorney had to get her off. Would the case go to trial?

Suddenly I had a horrible thought: if it did, I'd probably be called to testify. My name would come up. I didn't want the publicity, but I wouldn't have any choice.

What in the world could I say that wouldn't make things worse? How could I tell the world about our relationship, stupid as it seemed on the surface? What could I say with Anne in the audience?

Please, God, don't let this go to trial.

Since I'd had my relapse, I'd become quite familiar with a God of some sort who seemed to listen more attentively than old HP ever did.

Was that a man following me? Oh, for pete's sake, this is not the time for a mugging. What a lot of nerve, a mugging in a jail parking lot. I figured I had eighty dollars in my wallet, not enough to fight for, but too much to give up easily. I broke into a run for my car. What if he had a gun? I ran faster. Where was one of those guards when you needed them?

"Wait, wait up," the man yelled.

Sure, fella. I made it to my car and got the door unlocked before he was close enough to stop me. I made it inside, locked all doors, and poked the key wildly at the ignition.

The man was at my car. Rapping at my windows. I was afraid I'd pee, I was so terrified. And still mad at his nerve. The steel cab that had looked so safe when I was running toward it now felt like a tin can that could cave in at any moment. He could shoot me through the window. Dead for eighty dollars. Why couldn't I get the key in the lock? I wanted to scream. I tried to scream but my voice was a gargle in my throat.

"Wait up, I'm from the prosecutor's office," the man said. He went for his pocket and I said a prayer, certain I had seconds to live. When the shot didn't ring out I opened my eyes. He was showing me a gold shield and some kind of identification card through the window. It looked official. I breathed again.

I rolled down my window an inch and took it for

closer examination. Steven Gould, Deputy District Attorney. I compared his photo with the face peering through my window: pockmarks that a full beard couldn't totally hide. Yellowish eyes set deep in yellowish skin. High forehead, sparse wiry hair — probably another reason he had that beard, to prove he could still grow hair someplace. Beards make a lot of men look alike; it was the yellow eyes that made me believe the I.D. was official and open the door.

"What can I do for you, Mr. Gould?"

"You just visited Rhonda Rasmussen." He didn't need acknowledgment. "She told you what happened Saturday morning?" If it was true the phones were bugged, he didn't need acknowledgment on this point either. "Are you her friend?"

I debated answering him. Should I ask for a lawyer now? Probably not a good idea. Play it cool. "She needed help, and I was someone she thought of."

"Ah, yes. You're Priscilla Elaine Samms, and you have a liquor license for a bar called Samms', located on Hyperion in Silverlake. No outstanding tickets, no problems with any liquor violations. You used to be on the Governor's Commission on Alcoholism, under Brown. Partnership with Anne Nickolai, a licensed veterinarian, clinic on Sunset."

Don't drag Anne into this, I begged silently.

"So what do you want, Mr. Gould? You obviously checked me out when I applied to visit Rhonda."

"Call me Steve. That we did. Look, can we go somewhere to talk? Do you want to come inside? We can use the lawyers' consultation rooms."

"Are they bugged too?"

"What? Nothing's bugged here, ma'am."

My God, I'm a ma'am now. Maybe I should dye my hair again. I probably shouldn't talk to someone from the prosecutor's office; after all, he was the enemy. But the thought of Rhonda suffering in jail made me decide to do whatever I could to get her out ASAP. She was innocent. I could convince him of that, and he'd have the charges dropped. At the least, he'd convince the judge to let her out immediately on her own recognizance. She shouldn't be in that hellhole a minute longer. Probably nobody should. "If I'm supposed to call you Steve, call me Laney. I insist." I gave him a sweet smile, suiting a Priscilla, a smile my mother would have loved.

I got out of my car and accompanied Steve, walking without challenge past all the checkpoints that had held me up before. We detoured toward another building entirely, and we walked through a lobby with a huge oil painting, larger than life-size, of what had to be Mrs. Sybil Brand, socialite and founder of the Institute which was meant to improve jail conditions for women in L.A.

Some social welfare groups said that instead of improving, conditions had gotten worse, much worse, and that Sybil Brand was now a hellhole that should be torn down. I'd heard rumors that Mrs. Brand didn't even want her name associated with the jail anymore, though her picture still reigned in this lobby.

He showed me into a small room with a sofa covered with yellowed, cracked imitation leather, two stuffed easy chairs on either side of a scratched wood coffee table, and four plain wooden chairs, one on each side of a kitchen-size formica table. We took the easy chairs. He pulled out a pack of Camels. My old brand. "Do you mind?"

"It's your funeral," I said. After twenty years I could still want a cigarette. Probably not a good idea to alienate a man who held Rhonda's future in his hands. And mine too. But I was still angry at him for scaring me.

As if reading my mind, he apologized, "I'm sorry for the way I approached you a few minutes ago. I meant to be waiting for you when you left the visiting room, but I got called away." He lit up and moved an already-overflowing glass ashtray his way. "So . . . Laney. What do you know about this murder?"

"A lot less than you do. Just what Rhonda told me." I scrutinized his face to see how he would react to that statement.

"To be perfectly frank, it looks like self-defense from our side, too. But you can see, we have to check all angles."

I nodded. Try not to volunteer anything, I told myself. Maybe I should talk to Greene first. I said as much.

Steve smiled. "You're not being charged with anything, Laney. You're her friend. You want to help, don't you?"

Warning bells rang. Trust me, trust me. "Of course I do." I'd better not take a chance on messing things up. I gave him another Priscilla smile.

"Okay, I'm glad we agree on that. What I'm looking for, to be perfectly frank, is some evidence of Reverend Rasmussen's jealousy before he showed up at the cabin with a gun. Is there anything that comes to mind from your friendship with Ms. Rasmussen?"

I gave the appearance of thinking. "No, nothing I can think of." I'd definitely check with the attorney first.

"Did you ever meet Mr. Rasmussen?"

Was I being spied on when I was spying on Rhonda and her husband at church that day? Not likely. Nothing had happened yet. But be careful. "We never met."

"Ah." He tapped an ash into the full glass dish. A half-dozen butts promptly fell onto the coffee table.

Should I mention the beating? Did she say she'd told them about it? I remembered she did. So it should be safe to say that much. I chose my words carefully. "You know that he beat her a few days before he tracked her down to kill her."

His yellow eyes looked pained. "We can't quite say it that way until further investigation. Yes, it said in her statement that Dr. Rasmussen had hit her, which may explain the bruises. She said she'd come to you right after the beating, and you advised her to see an attorney."

"That's right. Did you check with the attorney?"

"Yes, we did. Not Mr. Greene, I recall. Another attorney, someone who primarily handled the Rasmussen finances. He didn't think too much of her story, as I recall. He couldn't believe that Dr. Rasmussen could have done such a thing. Frankly, that's the rub."

He paused for effect. Could he tell from my face that I wasn't going to say anything more? "Ms. Samms, I'd like you to think hard about anything that might help your friend, and give me a call, will you?" He pulled a card from his vest pocket. "Here's my office phone — give me a ring anytime. I'm on a beeper. Maybe you'll want to talk to Mr. Greene first and see if you can come up with anything. Anything, no matter how unimportant it may seem. I think we'll get to the truth of this matter, with a little help from Rhonda's friends." He stood up and extended his hand. "Thank you, Ms. Samms."

"You're welcome, Mr. Gould." I stood too, and at the door he turned to go a different direction than the one we'd followed coming in. I worried immediately how I would get out. "Do I need a pass or anything?" I called to his back.

"Don't worry, you've been noticed. The guards will be looking out for you on your way back to your car."

Gee, that was a relief.

Immediately upon returning home I called Randolph Greene. He was glad to hear I hadn't said anything to the prosecutor beyond the beating incident, and we made an appointment for first thing Wednesday morning. "I need to know the whole story, Laney. You can understand that."

"Sure." I gulped. How do I tell a man in Century City the whole story? He might even be straight. You never know.

Anne entered from the kitchen. "Carmen had a rough day today, had to call in Tim and Nancy both," she reported.

"Lots of sales?"

"Quite a bit — people want to see where Rhonda and Karen left for their tryst. You've had to notice, business has been down the past few months. Now it's booming. When the novelty wears off, it'll drop off again."

"It always falls during the holidays — people have better things to do." I shrugged. "We'll bring in a band, give a party, run a few ads. We'll get it back up again."

She meant since I hadn't been around as much. And she knew that I knew what she meant. We let it pass.

"So. How's Rhonda?"

"Better than you'd expect." I told her all about the visit, including the unexpected Mr. Gould. "On the way home I kept thinking about any evidence that the Rev was unbalanced. I'd give it to Randy Greene, of course. The beating should be enough, but apparently not in the law's eyes."

"Yeah? I'll try to think of anything else too."

"You'll do that?" I was surprised, thinking Anne would prefer to see Rhonda rot in jail.

"Sure. Nobody deserves Sybil Brand. Want some sour cream enchiladas?"

Anne was one terrific person. It felt like the good old days, sharing her great home cooking. But after dinner she retired to her room and read, while I watched sitcoms and moped. Radar kept me company, at least. What a dog.

Traffic into Century City was even worse than East L.A. the day before. Yuppie heaven was new high-rises, high rents, wide boulevards, a fashion mall right inside the complex, landscaping and fountains, and twenty-dollar-a-day underground parking lots. I got a ticket for validation and took the peach-paneled elevator to the twenty-second floor.

Randolph Greene looked like the Randolph Scott I remembered adoring in cowboy movies as a child. Tall, ruggedly handsome, sculpted chestnut hair, discreet pinstripes, wingtips, and a smile that could grace GQ. After a firm handshake, we entered an office of grays and burgundies, Berber rugs, a fourteen-foot-long conference table of black granite, and eggshell leather chairs that swallowed you up. I hoped Rhonda could get to her money to pay for all this.

Somehow, I liked the guy. I pictured him on a horse; it fit. So he was rich, so what. He was probably mortgaged up the kazoo to keep up this front. I still liked him.

I went through every detail of every meeting with Rhonda. Sure, I was embarrassed.

He took a lot of notes. When I'd finished, he tapped his Cross pen against the table top. "You talked about how this Lydia Munoz was shot by gangs on her way to meet Rhonda. Did the thought ever enter your mind that maybe it could have been Rhonda's husband?"

I was flabbergasted. "Never. How . . ."

"I don't know how. I want you to think about it. And the bullet into your house the day Rhonda came to see you — what if Rasmussen had followed her, and he shot into your house at you?"

Even in the climate-controlled office I got a chill. "How could . . ."

"Again, I don't know how, I'm just thinking aloud. Bear with me. Let's go over every detail of those two events again."

At home that night I went over the attorney's hypothesis with Anne. She was as horrified as I. "That means he could have killed you!"

"Looks that way," I had to agree. It didn't make me feel any too good.

She went to the kitchen and got the bullet from the drawer where she'd tossed it that night. "Take this to him, and see if he can do anything with it. Maybe it matches something. The bullets in Lydia."

"The bullets in Karen," I added grimly. I took the smashed-in cylinder — contact with a window and a wall had pretty much done it in — and put it in a baggie. "Forensics can do miracles these days. Maybe they will be able to find something."

All night long I worried and tossed in my bed, keeping Radar awake. She sensed my distress and kept padding outside and all around inside the house, sniffing and snorting. "Lemme at 'm," she all but said aloud.

When I finally fell asleep I dreamed scenarios far worse than anything on TV. In one I was lying on the floor, passed out drunk, and somebody sneaked in and picked me up and bashed my head against the counter edge.

In my dream I opened my eyes wide and saw the Reverend's face, pocked by wet red birdshot holes, as he picked me up again and smashed my head again and let me fall, my forehead dripping blood. The blood oozed into my mouth and I gulped and choked, the blood tasting like a sweet, thick white Russian.

I awoke instantly. It had been him. I woke Anne and told her. Neither of us could sleep anymore that night.

"No, I never saw his face, I didn't see anything, I was in and out of consciousness, near death from an alcohol overdose," I told Randolph the next morning. I also handed him the bullet.

"Ballistics will love this," he said. "I think it's possible you've saved your friend Rhonda. But it will take some time to analyze this and go through the proper channels. You'll be hearing from me soon."

Someone from ballistics called Samms' the next day and I met him at the house. He took a cursory look at the window and wall where the bullet had entered, measured some distances, and left within five minutes, long before Anne could arrive from the clinic. Somehow I'd wanted her there for the examination.

We decried the way the cops weren't taking this shooting any more seriously than they did the night we first reported it. Anne went back to work. I stayed home. The bar was not the most pleasant place for me to be these days. Carmen had gotten another raise through all of this.

The only meeting I could find for the afternoon was in Granada Hills; by the time I got there it was breaking up. Instead I called my sponsor at her job at Occidental. She met me at Denny's on Sunset when she got off.

"At first ballistics could find no link between the three crime scenes, but then they discovered the same gun was used with different barrels," Greene told me on Friday. "It's the bullet's path through the barrel which leaves the trajectory marks on it that the experts compare. Rasmussen had a Dan Wesson thirty-eight special revolver with a Pistol Pac that allowed him to switch sights, grips and barrels."

"I never heard of such a thing," I said. Women in the Army in the early sixties were given cursory training on the M16 assault rifle. Nobody expected we'd ever have to use one, or remember anything about it after basic training.

"Me neither, frankly. Guns are not my forte, though I've had to learn a lot as a criminal attorney. He had barrels in two-and-a-half-, four-, six-, eight- and ten-inch lengths, depending on his need. The small ones are better to hide, the longer ones have better stopping power. He even had a heavy bull barrel to cut down on recoil, and that's what he used on Lydia. The street was deserted. He could have driven up to her car and shot her point-blank."

"Maybe he wore his priest's collar," I speculated.

"Maybe," Greene said. "That would sure make her slow down if he tried to hail her car. You got the four-inch job, presumably because he hid the gun while he crept around your house, maybe concealing it in his pocket if anyone saw him."

I was suitably impressed.

"Police couldn't find any blood or skin on the edge of the counter at your bar, probably because that woman working for you is such a good housekeeper. She'd scrubbed that whole area to an inch of its life. But looking at the hospital records, it's clear your head hit something like a counter, and at a somewhat strange angle — you didn't fall outright. Nobody thought to look for anything out of the way before. He must have come to the bar after you'd made love with Rhonda, probably expecting to shoot you, and found you passed out. He probably decided on this less risky method instead. He took a few dollars and smashed a few things to make it look like teen vandalism. You should have died. He probably thought you had."

"Thanks," I said. "I needed to hear that. So why did a minister have all this stuff?"

"Oh, he wrote down it was for self-protection when he applied for his permit. Oh yes, the gun was registered. He took Rhonda to the shooting range once or twice, to show her how to use it. She told us all about it. She wasn't that good of a shot — records at the shooting range confirm it — but she could have shot a burglar at close range. The way things are these days, it's not out of line for a minister to own a gun, same as anybody else."

"Rhonda killed him with one shot."

"Sure, close up, with a twelve-gauge shotgun

loaded with double-ought birdshot. They're what a hunter uses for ducks, since not many hunters could hit a flying target high in the air with a single shot. A human at close range hasn't got a chance. He was a mess when police got there."

"Rhonda said there was blood everywhere when she tried to revive him."

"Yeah, she messed up the crime scene good. The prosecution called in a blood-spatter expert, but everything checked out anyway. Rasmussen fired one shot at her that ballistics found in the rear wall, then he turned and shot Karen twice, probably to be sure she was really dead. It was his second shot at Karen that gave Rhonda time to get the shotgun and fire first."

"You said a blood-spatter expert? What's that?"

"Somebody who measures how blood travels from gunshot wounds. They know how much momentum blood has coming out of different veins and arteries, and they know what kinds of spin blood picks up as a body falls. They study what kinds of patterns the blood makes when it hits walls, and whether there's anything that interrupts the expected flow — something that used to be there and was moved out of the way before police arrived, that kind of thing. It all checked out at the cabin."

He paused to make a note, then continued, "The police even checked on something called a death grip. Rasmussen didn't have the pistol in his hand when he was found, and he might have, since when someone dies they sometimes grab hold of anything in their hands with a super strong, so-called death grip. Especially when the victim dies suddenly and violently. Of course it doesn't always happen. But Rhonda said he'd dropped the gun when she took aim at him, and the experts finally agreed that she couldn't have stopped the momentum, once she'd started the motions to shoot him. Not in time anyway."

He leaned back in his mauve leather chair. "The evidence seemed clear enough that he was going to shoot Rhonda, too, and he dropped the gun at the last second only because he could see he was about to be shot." He smiled. "Police are satisfied — Rhonda's innocent."

"You mean she can go? Can I go get her?" I jumped up.

"No need. She's home already. Her San Marino neighbors may not have approved of her escort service, but I thought she should have a ride in the front seat this time."

She hadn't called. I was hurt, then relieved, then hurt.

"She should have the insurance money in a few days, and the bulk of the estate will be settled in a few months." Greene added, "Stuff in probate may take a few years."

At that I stopped. "There was a prenuptial agreement."

"Yes, there was, but it applied only to divorce. Once she was let go and all charges dropped, there was no reason for the bank to keep her from the community assets. She should get everything."

"It's none of my business, but how much are we talking about?" I couldn't help asking.

"Oh, the insurance was a half mil, he had two or

three million in other assets, stocks in the Rasmussen companies that she can convert right away, and we're still finding hidden assets. The house, of course, belonged to the church. The family is furious."

"I bet. They weren't too successful in keeping a lid on the publicity."

"Actually, they were. Without their influence, it could have been much worse. The Chandlers live in San Marino too." The Chandler empire includes the *Los Angeles Times* and numerous other media holdings.

I had to think about that one. I had to think about the whole thing. A lot.

"Thank you for all you've done," I said as I left.

"Don't thank me, you're the one who gave me the information that convinced the prosecution it was self-defense. Good job." Greene's handshake was a firm farewell.

I drove directly to Rhonda's. The yellow Mercedes was in the drive, but she didn't answer the doorbell. I called when I got home but no one answered the phone. I couldn't handle this. Like a crazed woman I drove back and nearly beat down her door.

"Rhonda," I screamed. "I know you're in there. I have to see you."

My hands hurt from pounding so hard. A neighbor, the woman quoted in the newspaper on how Rhonda was such a good neighbor, came out and glared at me. I didn't care.

"*Rhonda!*" I screamed.

The door cracked open as far as a guard chain allowed.

"Laney, I don't want to see you, I don't want to see anyone," she said, standing out of my reach.

"You have to see me, you have to," I insisted, desperate because I couldn't see her more clearly. I yanked on the chain in frustration.

"No I don't. Go away, Laney. Forget about me. I'm going to move away, someplace where nobody ever heard of the name Rasmussen or ever read the *L.A. Times*," she said. "I can't stay in L.A. anymore. My life is ruined here."

"You can't leave L.A. You're free now, you don't have a husband standing in your way," I begged.

"I'm free now. Maybe I'll go back home. Maybe I'll move someplace else on the coast, Seattle maybe, or San Diego. I don't know what I want to do. All I know is, I don't want to have anything to do with you or anybody." And she slammed the door firmly in my face.

"You're in shock, you don't know what you're saying," I yelled at the retreating footsteps. "Anybody'd feel the same, getting out of jail. You'll feel better tomorrow." I didn't believe it myself. There had been so much finality in Rhonda's voice.

I sat down on the cement walkway. It was cold on my rear through my jeans. I rocked back and forth, clasping my knees in front of me, burying my head between my legs.

It couldn't be true. I didn't know what was going through my head as far as the future was concerned, but I wasn't acting any too sane either. All I knew was that I wanted her. And she didn't want me.

I listened for sounds behind the door. The drapes

were drawn, and as I circled the entire house I could see nothing. Any more and I risked being arrested for trespassing, I finally realized, and I left.

I drove to the bar and went inside, waving away Carmen and Nancy. "Leave me alone," I warned them. They obliged, looking worriedly at each other. Nancy slipped away and made a phone call.

I played "She's Out of My Life" by Michael Jackson. Over and over again. I sat at the table we'd last sat at together and drank three cans of Diet Pepsi in a row. The few customers left.

When Anne came, I was ready to be taken home. I went to bed for three days straight. I was too tender, too raw, to handle all that had happened.

But I didn't drink.

CHAPTER THIRTEEN

You'd think I'd have had enough sense to give it up, especially since Anne was treating me like an almost-sane, almost-trustworthy individual again. But I kept agonizing over the whole thing, remembering every detail, trying to figure it all out.

Like a *Fatal Attraction* replay, I kept driving by Rhonda's house the next few weeks. She wouldn't answer the door. The black BMW her husband had favored disappeared, then her yellow Mercedes had a "For Sale" sign on it, and then it was gone, too. Frequently trucks were in the drive, taking away a piano, boxes of books, desks and office equipment. I didn't stop whenever I could see anyone else was there.

One day I pulled up and caught a glimpse of yellow moving in the rose garden. I tiptoed through the paths leading to the garden and surprised her. "My God," she said, dropping shears and rosebuds into the dirt.

"Here, let me help." I bent over to pick them up.

"Don't touch me. I'll call the police."

"Hey, no need." I put my hands in the air to show I was innocent. "I had to see you, that's all."

"So now you've seen me, and you can go home." She picked up the scissors and a handful of the roses and headed for the rear door of the house.

"Rhonda, you aren't treating me right. I'm the one who got you off. Your attorney said so."

The words meant nothing to her. I caught her at the door. Her face was inches from mine. I kissed her. Cold. Then a flush of warmth. She reached up with the hand holding the scissors and held me close. The roses fell from her hands. It was going to be all right.

"Oh, Laney, thank you for sticking by me through this horrible time. Maybe later . . ." Her body stiffened again. "But now I have to be alone. I have to get out of here. Out of this house. Out of this town. Away from you and everybody." She wrestled loose, waving her scissors wildly, and slammed the door on me. She was stronger than I remembered. That dancer's body.

I was in shock. She really didn't want me.

"You don't have to leave town. We can build a

life here," I said as loudly as I could at the door without chancing the neighbors' hearing. "This is L.A. Anything goes. People have short memories. You don't want to go to Seattle or San Diego or any of those dreary places. We can make a home together here." Total silence from inside.

I sat down on her doorstep like a fool, trying to figure out what went wrong. She had to still be recovering from the murders, that's all. What was that condition?

"Rhonda? Did you ever hear of post-traumatic-stress syndrome? You're probably suffering from that. You should see a counselor. I know this great woman, she helped . . ." Don't say she helped Anne and me on our problems. "She helped a lot of women I know. She's excellent. You'd love her. Open the door and we'll talk about it."

Silence.

"I'll come by every so often and talk about it some more. Can I leave the name of this counselor on the door?"

I debated writing down Dr. Stern's name and phone number. Why not? Rhonda might come to her senses and give her a call. I wrote it on the back of a Broadway bill-payment envelope I had in the car and tucked it in the door.

"If you won't talk to a counselor, at least you should talk to somebody. You can talk it all out with me. I'm the one who knows the most about what's happened. It'll help you to go over all the details and work it out of your system. Maybe we can figure out all the loose ends, like how did Charles find out about your plans for the cabin? Why didn't he kill me the night at the bar? Did he really listen in on your phone calls? Did you know he had that big black Chevy he drove to my house, and what happened to it?"

More silence. Then Rhonda, from just inside the door, said, "Charles was a very smart man. I'm sure he double-checked everything, so what's to gain from hashing things over and over?"

I could sense her body on the other side of the thick door, almost as I could sense heat from her hand through the glass at Sybil Brand.

"Laney, please understand. I need to get away. Maybe I'll feel like calling you, later, when I can. Please . . . for now . . . just let me be." Then I heard her rushed footsteps heading for someplace else in the house.

Reluctantly, I left, taking with me one of the yellow roses she'd dropped. The lady wanted to be alone. She definitely needed to talk, but it would take time. She'd call me. Maybe. I wasn't so sure.

Still, I drove by a few days later. The envelope was still stuck in the door. I crumpled it and put it in my pocket. No sense leaving sensitive words like that around for the meter reader. I had the distinct feeling the house was vacant already, even though there were signs of occupancy — garden shears left out to rust in the rain, an open yellow umbrella that had dried off long ago flopping around the yard. Strange. I didn't go back again. The yellow rose that I'd left on my dashboard crumbled and disintegrated.

Life without Rhonda was dull. Business was down at Samms', but I splurged on a set of gourmet copper cookware for Anne for Christmas. We always celebrated our anniversary on Christmas, since neither of us could agree exactly on when we did start going together. This one would have been our twentieth. Now it was just Christmas.

She bought a tree and I put it up and strung lights and garlands, same as always, while she put on the ornaments. It was the most beautiful tree we'd ever had. But then we say that every year.

We unwrapped presents early Christmas Eve. She told me to go outside and get in my pickup to check out her present to me — a new stereo system, to replace the one stolen out of the cab a year or more ago. *The Magic Flute* started playing the moment I turned the key. She made *molé poblano* for our dinner in the cookware. We were careful not to touch as we maneuvered the gift exchange.

Rob had called from Palo Alto — he'd met a girl and wasn't coming home this year. Anne talked to him for an hour on the phone. I'd been wondering how we'd swing the bedroom situation if he'd vacationed with us. The sofa isn't too comfortable.

For Christmas Eve at the bar I'd hired an unknown women's band that had auditioned like Cris Williamson in her first rocking years. That night they sounded like Weird Al Yankovich. Lots of couples left early.

I was tied into this group for New Year's Eve too, and it was too late to get another group. I chewed them out and told them to shape up for New Year's. They were better that night but not great.

Anne spent New Year's Eve at the bar with me, both of us trying to ignore the fact that the joint was half-full.

At midnight the band played a raucous updated version of "Auld Lang Syne" and Anne kissed me delicately, our first kiss in many a month. It was a dry and distant kiss. I held her close on the dance floor and cried. I think she cried a little too.

When the offer came from the real estate developers in March, we couldn't believe it. Sure, Hyperion was booming all around us, and we'd seen perfectly lovely single family homes on decent lots replaced with luxury condos.

Very nice small businesses had come and gone, each one an upgrade of the one before. A new strip mall down the street was a gleaming monstrosity of hot pink, maroon and royal blue neon against white pseudo-Spanish architecture. The mall featured such yuppie trademarks as fat-free luxury yogurt joints and The Sharper Image.

The developers wanted to put a similar strip mall on our block, and each business owner had received an inflated proposition, hard to refuse. All of us met over lunch at the vegetarian corner deli and talked about it.

None of us wanted to leave. What would we do? We couldn't afford to buy new businesses in L.A., the way prices keep going up. We vowed to hold out together.

With the pressure of that offer hanging over us, Anne and I began to fight over bills. Actually, I was making some extra money on the side from Kitt Meyers, a hotshot in women's music. Kitt liked the public relations stuff I did for the bar, and she recommended the UCLA Extension public relations sequence to me, to sharpen the skills I didn't know I had. I'd already started the first class, in newsletter design. Kitt showed me how to use my laptop computer to do a lot more with my little newsletter for Samms', and now I was doing a newsletter to the record stores which carry women's music as well.

The full-time fund-raiser for AIDS Aid had died, and instead of hiring someone new, they started paying me to do a little more of the same things I'd done before for them. After all, I'd gotten them the grant so they could start to pay some of the staff a living wage. So money wasn't the real issue when Anne chose to pick these fights.

I could see another one was coming when she started getting our tax stuff together for the accountant. She had boxes of papers home from the bar and her clinic, and she was grumbling over every dollar she thought we'd wasted the past year.

I was spending too much for imported beers; all the overtime to Carmen really added up; paper towels had gone up exorbitantly. "That stupid phone in your back office really cost us a mint. You should have replaced it the moment you realized it didn't hang up right sometimes. Look at these old phone bills. You couldn't have talked for two hours, three hours. My God, this call is nearly two hundred dollars! You paid it without wondering?"

I couldn't believe it and scanned the bills myself. True, I'd had to replace the cordless phone because its connections became more and more irregular. I'd try to make a call and the batteries would be dead after only a few weeks, at ten dollars a pop for a new battery pack. The reception on it hadn't been that great, either. But two hundred dollars? $197.43 to be exact.

I didn't recognize the phone number. It wasn't any of my distributors that I called a lot. Idly I dialed the number from the phone next to the sofa, just to see who I'd allegedly talked to for all those minutes.

"Crystal Lake Conference Center," the voice answered.

Huh? I hung up.

I'd never called any Crystal Lake Conference Center. Not many other people have access to the back apartment at the bar. I couldn't imagine Carmen or Nancy or Tim having any reason to call a conference center. I checked the bill again for more information.

The call was placed at 6:22 p.m. the Friday before Thanksgiving. Dimly I tried to remember who was there, who could have called Crystal Lake.

A shudder passed over me. Rhonda. She and Karen's stopover to gloat about their vacation. And Charles was at a conference in Crystal Lake.

Why would Rhonda have called her husband? To say hello and wish him a happy weekend? To remind him to bring home some toilet paper on his way home? To let him think she was at home missing him?

"Who was it to?" Anne asked.

"Crystal Lake Conference Center."

"Crystal Lake?" I could see her going through the same possibilities I had. She took the bill back from me. "That was when Rhonda and Karen were here." She made a "humph" sound. "Knowing Mrs. Preacher, she probably called him and said, 'Meet us at the cabin for a threesome.' "

"Stop it, Anne."

She looked at me sharply.

"Bitchiness doesn't become you," I said. We went on to argue about the electric bill.

The reminder of Rhonda set the juices flowing again. I mentally kicked myself all the way over to the San Marino house and watched some children scream their way through hopscotch on the sidewalk. A new minister's family lived there. No more reason to visit San Marino.

Taking a different route back to help break the cycle, I spied Page One bookstore. Maybe a good lesbian romance would take my mind off things. Maybe the latest issue of *On Our Backs* for good old lesbian erotica. More likely I should read something heavy and political. Or a self-help pop psychology manual.

"Hi, Laney." The sales clerk greeted me like an old friend. I recognized her from her frequent visits to Samms', but I couldn't remember her name. How embarrassing. Happens all the time. Rather than admit she hadn't made that much of an impression on me, I decided to wing it.

"Hi, read any good books lately?" I'm so witty. She escorted me to the new books section and pointed out a few. I wandered around for a while and picked up the latest L.A. *Lesbian News.*

"Your friend sure loved that article on you," the clerk said. "She read the whole thing standing right where you're standing now, and she asked a few more questions about you too. I'm the one who gave her directions to Samms'." She looked proud, then slightly uneasy. "After what happened to her, you probably wish I'd never sent her over."

"Who do you mean?" I was afraid I knew.

"That Rasmussen woman. The one who killed her husband. You had a thing with her, didn't you?"

Carmen wasn't the only one with an ear for gossip.

"Which article was that?"

"You know, the big one the *LN* wrote about you and Anne and how you were practically pioneers in the L.A. lesbian scene. I wondered after I read it if you and Anne would stick together, and then this Rasmussen woman came in and I knew you'd had it. She was hot for you, that's for sure. She tried to look cool about it, but I could tell she was really interested in that article. I watch how the eyes dilate — it's a trick I learned at a workshop on closing the sale."

I processed this information.

"Whatever happened to her anyway?" the clerk asked.

"She left L.A. after she was released. She got a lot of money when he died."

"Ummm. So where'd she go?"

"Haven't a clue."

"Ummm." Apparently deciding she'd pushed her luck, she withdrew to behind the counter again.

My mind couldn't quite take in these new facts. So Rhonda already knew all about me when she'd come into Samms' that first night. She knew about Anne, and that the relationship was in trouble.

I picked up a couple of novels and magazines and went to the counter. "What else did she buy, do you remember?"

"Sure, she bought a whole bunch of books. This one on coming out. *The Joy of Lesbian Sex.* Something on AA."

A faint memory stirred. I thumbed through the coming-out stories and found the one I wanted, about the woman who first knew she was a lesbian when she was on the school playground with a girl she had a crush on, and another friend started talking about the Isle of Lesbos.

I knew right away I was one of those kinds of women, and it scared me to death, so I became boy-crazy to hide it, the chapter stated. Almost identical to what Rhonda said when I asked how she'd first known she was a lesbian.

"Thanks, I appreciate the information," I told the clerk. I didn't have enough cash on me to pay for all the books and had to leave one behind. Far more embarrassing than not remembering the clerk's name. And I'd already gotten out the max from the ATM for the day. What would the rumors say about my finances by tomorrow?

Who cared? Life stinks. I could go no further into thinking about what the new information meant than that.

But these new facts dug at me. At the bar, I called Randolph Greene and told him what I'd learned.

After a long silence, he said only, "What do you want me to do about it?"

"I don't know. I just wanted to tell somebody. What do you make of it?"

"The case is closed. I did my job. She left town already, didn't she?"

"New people were in the house last time I went by. Do you know where she went?" I asked.

"She's supposed to call me with her new address, so she can get the rest of her money when probate clears. That'll take a couple of years, though. Our business is concluded — her check cleared." He chuckled.

"Say, what was her maiden name, can you tell me?"

"Sorry, that would be confidential."

"Did you talk to her parents?"

"Yes, I did, but I can't tell you anything more."

Vaguely I remembered the newspaper article with the interview with her parents. "Umm, they were Jacksons, from Backdraft, Pennsylvania."

"You didn't hear it from me."

"That's true. Thanks a lot, Mr. Greene. I'll let you know if I find out anything else."

"What do you think you'll find out, Ms. Samms?"

"I don't know."

"Maybe I'd rather not know either."

"Do you really expect she'll send you an address to get the rest of the money from probate?"

"Depends on whether three million is enough for what she has in mind, doesn't it?" He gave off a loud sigh on the other end of the line. Click. *Prick.*

Anne wanted to know what was wrong when she came in to the bar after work that afternoon. For some reason I told her. I guess I needed any input I could get.

She was equally puzzled. "You've still got her under your skin, don't you?"

"Maybe a little. I don't know why." Anne was cool after this exchange, and she went home soon after. There was no dinner in the fridge when I got home.

CHAPTER FOURTEEN

I couldn't sleep that night and while I tossed I made plans for a little trip. Anne grumbled about finances, but she saw I had to do this. We both needed to know.

Driving three thousand miles was out of the question. I called my friendly local lesbian travel agent and got the best deal on coach fare to Philly, with two days' free rental car thrown in. I got my heaviest jacket dry-cleaned and bought heavy socks and a wool scarf with matching gloves.

Meanwhile, I studied my Rand McNally atlas and

found Pennsylvania phone books at the library. I copied the page with Jacksons on it from Backdraft. There were four families, and a Jackson Car and Truck Repair. I remembered the paper had called Rhonda's father a mechanic. Not a farmer. There was no Horseshoe in Pennsylvania.

The navy Cavalier at Budget smelled like cherry cough syrup — I noticed that the floor mat was sticky where my heel rested — and jazz blared out at me when I switched on the radio. As I drove northwest from Philly, only country-western stations came in.

A postcard from the one drug store in Backdraft claimed that the village got its name from a forest fire that raged over that area of Pennsylvania in the late 1700s. Some farmers were caught in a backdraft when the wind changed, leading to immortality for the event via the name.

Otherwise, Backdraft was known for its hunting, fishing and beautiful fall colors. It wasn't exactly ugly in early spring, either. The name of the brilliant yellow bushes which bloomed everywhere in my Michigan childhood popped into my head: forsythia. How I'd loved forsythia, the first color of spring. Every house had a bed of hyacinths and crocuses where there was shade, tulips if the bed was sunny.

Old women walked the streets and didn't look around to see who might be following them. Kids played in front yards without an adult watching. Shaggy dogs ambled across the streets and cars honked and slowed rather than try to hit them. The corner bank looked as solid as its ivy-covered brick, though that could be deceiving. Centerpiece of the town was Hochman's Department Store, as large as a Sears.

Outside of town, farmers on tractors made fresh furrows through the black dirt, white seagulls following closely behind to seize the upturned worms and grubs. The IGA advertised eggs for seventy-nine cents a dozen. Last I'd noticed in L.A., they were twice that.

The tiny library had a dozen kids' bikes on a rack outside, with no chains or locks. If I'd been Rhonda, I wouldn't have left. Yes, I would, what was I thinking about, I'd left the midwest ASAP myself. Any ambitious young person would. Maybe the lucky ones find a way to go back. It would mean being back in the closet — would I do that again? Probably not. Only white-bread people? Forget it. Regretfully I shelved that line of thought.

Jackson Car and Truck Service was on the main street, called, appropriately, Main Street. "Est. 1892," read the cornerstone of the brick station. A half-dozen cars were in various stages of repair, up on hydraulic lifts and jacks, hoods up, cables running to and fro.

"What can I do ya for?" asked a man with a backward-turned baseball cap embroidered "Milt." He looked the right age, maybe fifty-something. His greasy workshirt and jeans were a typical mechanic's, complete with butt crack when he bent over to check a cable on his way over to me. He offered me a grease-encrusted hand. I took it and afterward discreetly wiped my hand off on a tissue in my pocket.

"What's acting up?" he motioned toward the Cavalier.

"Nothing, knock on wood." I smiled my most ingratiating smile. My Priscilla smile. "My name is Laney Samms, and I'm a friend of your daughter Rhonda's. From L.A."

I'd learned from a Perry Mason show to go ahead and say the relationship you suspect. If I'd asked if he was Rhonda's father he could have denied it, or denied knowing her, or he could have been put off guard by the question. Making it sound as if I already knew he was her father, I might get lucky. Assuming he really was her father.

Close. He turned cool but said, "You want my brother, Al. He's in back." He gestured toward a rear workroom where a wiry short man was muttering and all but tearing his red hair out over a ledger. Bookkeeping. I sympathized.

Gingerly stepping over the cables and tools on the cement floor, I headed for Al. Milt eavesdropped openly.

"Hi, Mr. Jackson. My name is Laney Samms, and I'm a friend of your daughter's from Los Angeles."

Another headache, his body language said. "So?" his vocal cords said.

"I was at a business meeting in Philadelphia and I thought I'd drive out and see her. She said she might be moving back here."

"She never came back here." Al stood up, reluctantly. When he saw how I towered over him, he had to regret it. "Whatcha want her for?"

"Nothing special, I just thought I'd look her up. Any idea where she did move?"

"She wouldn't tell us nothin'." His gaze was frank, if hostile. "What's your relationship to Rhonda?"

If only you knew. I grimaced inside. "We're friends. I knew her and her husband at the church."

"Terrible thing, that." Al scratched his hair, the same kind of natural curls Rhonda was endowed with. "You knew him, too?"

"Only a little." Don't get caught in your own lies, I warned myself. "She's a wonderful person."

Milt snickered behind me. Al looked at me quizzically.

"Wonderful person, eh? Look, Mrs. Samms, I don't have nothin' to tell ya. Maybe you want to go by the house, see what the missus might say."

Exactly what I'd hoped. "Where do you live?"

"Forester, up past the light two blocks and left a quarter mile to the Henley farm and turn right at the next corner. We're the second house on the left."

"Excuse me, which way is 'up'? And how will I know the Henley farm?"

He walked with me to the road and looked right. "See the light?" he patronized me. There was only one light in town, flashing yellow in all four directions.

"Yes," I said, an obedient Priscilla.

"Go two blocks past that and turn left. Go a quarter mile to a farm that says Henley on the barn in big white letters. A couple hundred feet after that will be a corner. Go right. We're at one-twenty Forester, a red brick house on the left side of the road."

"Thank you very much," I said.

Mrs. Jackson answered the door herself. I guessed it was her because she was even shorter than her husband, and she had Rhonda's blue-green eyes. Her short permed hair was a natural pale blonde tinged with silver.

"Hello, I'm Laney Samms, and your husband said you might be able to tell me a little more about where Rhonda might have moved. I'm a friend of hers from Los Angeles."

She rolled her eyes and left the door open as she headed to the kitchen, motioning with a wave of a dishtowel that I was to follow.

Inside, a soap was on the 45-inch television. She was rolling out pie crust. A home-canned quart of cherries stood on the table. An empty package of Virginia Slims lay crumpled in a Holiday Inn ashtray.

"Ma, who is it?" a male voice yelled from upstairs.

"Nobody you need to know nothin' about," she said, her voice barely raised. Another red head, this time attached to a gangly young man in a black Boyz II Men sweatshirt and torn jeans, leaned over the railing.

"Ma-ah," he bleated in that two-syllable way teenagers have. "What'd you say?"

"I said it's nothin' that concerns you." The mother sounded annoyed. The young man, whose face looked older than he acted, maybe 20 or 22, galloped down the pine stairs and plunked himself on a worn couch, looking at me expectantly. He must have learned his open eavesdropping from his uncle, or maybe it was a family tradition.

"Billy, get upstairs," Mother ordered him. Son ignored her. She only sighed and turned to me. "What do you want?"

"Nothing, I only wanted to keep in touch with her, and she moved pretty quickly — after . . ." What words do I use to describe the mess?

She didn't want me to finish the sentence anyway, she knew what I meant. "I don't know where she went. I'm sorry I can't help."

My frustration mounted; she was my last resort. "Did she ever mention where she might move to? She'd said San Diego, or Seattle, or back here."

"Well, she certainly didn't come here." Mother shrugged. "I don't have any idea whether she went to one of those other places you mentioned."

"Did she have any other friends around here, someone she might have gotten in touch with?"

"No, not that I know of. She left us all behind when she met that minister fella."

What do I ask now? "Umm." I filled time. "Was there any special city where she liked to visit? Did she like to go to New York? Or anyplace else?"

She carefully considered the possibilities. "No, none that I can think of. She never went traveling none when she was here. She wasn't married then."

"What did she do before she went to Philadelphia to nursing school?" I was running out of options.

"Nothing much," she said. "You know, dated a few boys, worked for the Hochmans, helped Dad do the books at the shop."

"Is there any boy she dated that she might have contacted since . . ."

"No, they all up and married good girls, live around here, have families. She'd have nothing to do with the likes of them."

"Oh yes, she did. She was gonna marry Clyde, but she went to school instead," Billy interjected.

"I said, shut up!" Mrs. Jackson yelled.

I became aware that Billy was prancing in his seat, keeping his lips tightly together with obvious effort, his eyes dancing at me. What did he really want to tell me? Maybe I could get him outside. Meanwhile, I continued with his mother, asking anything I could think of.

"Did she have any hobbies?"

"No, she liked to play around with flowers. Always loved pink roses, as I recall."

"Yellow, Ma, she loved yellow roses," Billy said. "Remember how we used to tease her with that old song?" He fairly bounced, pulling at his lower lip.

"Hush up, child, don't stick your nose in where you're not wanted."

I began to wonder if Billy was slightly retarded. His youthful outbursts didn't match his mature face. Mrs. Jackson saw me staring at him, and disapproval set in her mouth. I wasn't supposed to notice. Maybe I needn't bother talking to him. I looked back at Mrs. Jackson and gave her a Priscilla smile.

"You must have been very proud of her when she married and helped her husband with such a fine church in L.A."

"I suppose so," Mother said. "Never did get out there to see it. The church in Bucks County neither. Not that she asked us to come."

"What kind of a girl was she?" I was desperate to keep her talking, to not abandon my last resource.

"Look, Mrs. Samms, I don't know what you want, but I don't think I can answer any more of your questions. None of us saw Rhonda in many years, and this trouble she was in came as quite a shock.

You understand. Now, if you'll excuse me." She picked up the rolling pin again. It didn't look menacing in her hands, but I took it as a signal. The conversation definitely was over.

"Sorry to have bothered you, Mrs. Jackson. Thank you for all your help. I'll see myself out."

I was bitterly disappointed. Nothing she'd said had helped me at all. Now what could I do?

Billy suddenly appeared at my car window. I hadn't heard him behind me. "Hi," he said, his badly cut red hair bobbing down in his eyes in uneven strands. He saw me looking at his head. "Do you like my haircut? I did it myself. I think I look like Ozzie Osbourne, don't you?"

"I can see a resemblance," I smiled. Without asking he got into my car.

"Now listen, Billy, you'd better get out. Does your mother know you're out here?" Could she still hear me over the soap if I had to yell?

"Naw, I snuck out. You wanna know a secret? I saw Rhonda, with Clyde."

"When?" My heart raced.

"About a year ago. She had a yellow convertible, and she had Clyde in the car with her. She wanted to say goodbye to me. She told me not to tell anybody, but I want to tell you. Is that okay?"

"Yes, Billy, it's okay. What did she say?"

"Not much. She just said she wanted to see me one last time, and she told me not to believe anything anybody said about her."

"Was Clyde going away with her?"

"I don't know. I don't think so. He didn't look like he was too happy. I was happy to see her."

"I bet you were, Billy. You seem like a very nice boy to me. I bet you were her favorite brother."

He beamed. "She liked me, and I liked her."

"Tell me exactly what she said and did when you saw her, Billy."

"I told you everything." We both sat with this information. Finally he said, "You want to know more about Rhonda? I'll show you her hangouts."

My hopes rose again. "Sure, Billy. Where do we go?"

"I like to drive. Can I drive for you?" He leaned over to grab the steering wheel.

"Sorry, Billy, this is a rental car. Only I can drive it, otherwise I get in trouble."

"Oh, okay." He pouted, then giggled. "Drive down to the Henley farm and turn left, back to town. Did you see our town when you came in?"

"Yes, I did, Billy, and it's a very nice town."

"Rhonda hated it. She always said she had to get away. She always wanted to be rich. She said she'd do it, too. I believed her. Rhonda always did what she said she'd do."

"Okay, Billy, we're heading into town. Now which way?"

"Turn left at the light, the other way from Dad's shop." I followed his directions and the homes got larger. We reached the ultimate, what had to be called a mansion.

A curved stone wall more than eight feet tall wound around a landscaped lot at least a city block square. Two carved stone lions guarded the locked wrought-iron gate over the opening. Behind the wall could be seen a huge three-story stone home decorated with a turret, widow's walk and Victorian gingerbread. Several smaller outbuildings the size of ordinary homes dotted the grounds. A freshly painted white sign announced, "Hochman Home for the Aged."

"That used to be the Hochmans' house, but they all died and the home got sold for taxes," Billy informed me. "Some big city outfit bought the store. Rhonda did housekeeping for the Hochmans after school. She loved this place, talked about it all the time. She'd talk about the knickknacks. Sometimes she'd make believe they were hers. Once in a while she stole something, brought it home and showed it to me. Mom found her stash one day and made her bring it back, and then she didn't work for the Hochmans no more. I guess they fired her, do you think?" He looked worried, even now. "It's not good to get fired."

"No, it's not," I agreed.

"Rhonda liked me best, I didn't make fun of her for liking rich stuff. I liked the things she brought home too. She always said she was gonna marry a rich man and live in a palace. She wanted to marry Clyde, but she decided she was gonna marry a doctor, 'cause doctors are rich."

"So this was her favorite place in town?"

"One of 'em," Billy confided. "Now go down this road to the creek, and turn down the dirt road till I tell you."

We came to a rolling hill that paralleled the road. "Pull over there under that tree," Billy ordered.

For a second I wondered if I should have trusted

him. It was awfully remote. He was almost as tall as I am and probably stronger.

"See that path? Rhonda liked to walk along the creek, where nobody could see her. Nobody knew where to look, and even if they drove right down this road they'd never find her. She liked to sit down here by the creek and practice her target shooting."

I froze. "Her target shooting?"

"Yeah, Dad made us all learn how to shoot, even the girls. Rhonda was the best shot of all, but being a girl and all, she didn't get much chance to show off. My brother Eddie was good, too, not as good as her, and he got to win all kinds of prizes in ROTC. When she started to go out with Clyde she didn't come here anymore. Can you shoot a rifle?"

"I've shot a few guns in my day. Not lately," I admitted. Basic training was a long time ago.

"Dad don't like me to shoot none. He thinks I don't know how to handle guns good enough. You got a gun I can shoot?" His freckles made red polka dots through his tan. He was eager to get out and fire something, anything. I remembered how my first gunshot threw my shoulder back and left bruises for days. I remembered that one of Charles's interchangeable pistol barrels, the one used on Lydia, was designed for less recoil.

"No, Billy, I don't have any guns. I think we'd better get back now."

"Awww." But he settled down in his seat and rambled on about the woodchuck we saw alongside the road and how good raccoon meat was and how he was gonna go coon hunting himself someday, and how his father wouldn't let him work at the shop, and he didn't know what kind of job he would get someday. If anybody did hire him, you can bet he wouldn't get himself fired.

He wished he could go to school but there wasn't any more school for him, and he got pretty bored all day and he sure missed Rhonda. If I found her, would I say hello for him, and ask her when she was coming back?

I let him off at his house with more thanks and drove to the airport, troubled by my thoughts.

CHAPTER FIFTEEN

More and more furious as each piece of the puzzle slipped into place, I put it all together on the plane. Now all I had to do was convince the authorities. I called Steven Gould from LAX.

His office smelled of cigarettes and overflowed with papers on every inch of surface and floor. His weird yellow eyes watched me as if I were a mouse within striking range.

I told him all that I had learned about Rhonda's skill with guns, about her lies, about her knowing about me from the *LN* article, about her lifting words from a book for her own background, and most of all about the phone call to the Crystal Lake Conference Center.

"You've had longer to think about it. What do you think really happened?" Gould challenged me.

"Obviously, I don't know. There's no way anybody can know except Rhonda, and she's disappeared. But on the way home I thought out some possibilities."

"Such as?"

"Hear me out now. What if she really was motivated by money, the way her brother said she was? She scoped me out. She could have researched Rasmussen at the hospital in Philly, scion of a wealthy family, richer than any doctor. Harvard grad, mining money, the whole thing. She marries him. The pre-nup grinds at her, but she bides her time, plotting for a way to get rid of him and get the money. All these hate crimes against gays start and she comes up with the idea of using homophobia and jealousy to provide an alibi."

"So you don't think she was really a lesbian?" Gould interjected.

I told him about Billy, and about Clyde. "Suppose she wasn't a lesbian. She didn't have a coming-out story of her own — she got one from a book. The first moment you realize you're gay is traumatic. You don't forget."

His hand made a circular motion. "Get on with it."

"So suppose she starts to read up on lesbianism at Page One and she comes across the article on me and Anne and bells start to go off in her head. She comes into the bar a few times just to watch, to see if she could set me up."

"And she could."

"She could." I frowned. "In any event, she comes up with the idea of setting up a stooge —" I hated to use the word about myself. "After all, Randolph Greene said it himself — I was the one most responsible for getting her off because of the information I gave. Information she fed me."

"Any reason why she picked Lydia and Karen?"

"I was trying to think of something. Maybe it was random. Maybe it fit with the story she fed me about wanting a baby, and they were both mothers, even though their kids didn't live with them. You could check with USC and see if she ever went through their test tube program — she said she did."

He wrote a note to himself.

"Actually, that part doesn't matter. What matters is that she's read the *LN* article on Anne and me, and she's no dummy, she reads between the lines that Anne and I are having troubles. I probably said something stupid about the desire for more excitement in my life, about a long-term relationship inevitably becoming, well, boring. I probably wasn't quite that blunt, but she learned enough to push all my buttons."

I gave him an edited version of my rationale of Rhonda's superior performance in bed. The sex was fantastic, but it could have been fueled more by the adrenaline of deceit and high-stakes planning, creating tension that was beyond what normally comes out of "normal" sex. If straight women can fake exciting sex to keep a man, why not to keep a woman? I'd faked once or twice myself, I had to admit to myself.

"Get on with it," Gould repeated, ignoring my burning face.

"She leaves me in place as stooge, and sights her first victim, Lydia Munoz. She must have scouted out that Riverside Drive deserted location for the shooting and told Lydia to go that way for some reason, or maybe it's Lydia's usual route home."

"That yellow Mercedes would stick out like a sore thumb," Gould interrupted.

"Yeah, I thought about that. Maybe she had another car stashed someplace, maybe the big old Chevy like the one that Anne saw at our house, what we decided Charles must have driven. Maybe she had a wig, or a hat, something to make her look like a gang member, in case she was spotted."

"You're really stretching," Gould said.

"I know, but hear me out. Say Rhonda used the big barrel with the least recoil because she was out of practice with guns, or maybe she'd driven out to the desert and found a practice spot like her childhood shooting range."

"Not impossible to imagine," Gould admitted. "She downplayed her shooting skills the times Charles took her to a range to 'teach' her." He looked at me skeptically. "So she shot at you through the window from this old Chevy?"

"Remember, she came to my house first. She could have hidden in the brush around our house. Silverlake's full of all sorts of chaparral that she could hide in."

He nodded. "So she uses a different gun barrel,

just in case police compare bullets, as if whoever shoots at you is deliberately out to mislead the police. But at the same time she was quick to tell us about Rasmussen's gun kit with the extra barrels and sights."

"I'd thought of that myself. So the next time she makes a move is when I'm passed out drunk in the bar. She probably could have killed me by hitting my head harder on the counter — she was stronger than she looked — and maybe she would have, if I had opened my eyes."

"She still needed you, and you didn't open your eyes, so she let you live."

"Right. She still needed her stooge."

He twisted in his cracked leather chair. "She could have beaten herself up with a baseball swinging on a tether — I've seen other cases like that. We found a broken mirror on the wall of her house and it had shreds of skin on it — one of the points that convinced us she'd been beaten. But you'd be surprised at what people will do to mutilate themselves to escape conviction. I've seen it all."

"I bet you have." I handed it to him. "Naturally, Rhonda shows off her bruises to her stooge."

"She timed this alleged beating so that the bruises would still show, and they wouldn't be old enough to be mistaken for any new bruises the night of the shooting," he continued, concentrating. "So how do you explain the shooting at the cabin?"

"That's a bit harder to figure out, since the blood-spatter evidence had to fit. She was a nurse, so she may have learned about blood spattering as a forensic tool."

"Doubtful. Maybe she read up on it. There's a lot

of stuff in the average public library on how to commit the perfect crime, at least on how people have tried. She certainly knew how to do her research."

I gave a bitter smile back at him. "All right, say she shot Karen first, and it took two shots. She'd wear gloves and use the pistol, and she'd shoot from the doorway."

"So the ballistics paths would be right."

"Right. So when Charles came up the path, probably expecting a wonderful night of lovemaking to relieve his religious conference, she nailed him with the shotgun as he came in the door."

"And then she fell on his body to see if he was alive — and at the same time to make a mess of the crime scene and spread the gunpowder residue around," Gould mused.

"She'd have to lift his body a few feet to get his hand at waist level, so that the impact in the wall behind her would be from the correct angle," I continued. "She'd have had to clean off his hand to put the pistol in it for this shot. He needed to have gunpowder on his hands to prove he'd done the shooting, and no blood on his palms where it wouldn't have spattered with the gun in place."

"No problem there — did you know that the shot hit his hand the worst, blew it clean off?"

I hadn't. "I'd been trying to figure out how she'd plan for the possibility he'd wear gloves, and how she'd get his fingerprints on the gun if he hadn't shot it . . ."

"His fingerprints were on the gun, all right — he probably was the last to use it without gloves.

Rhonda's a sharp cookie, she'd use gloves all the way."

I remembered Rhonda behind her door, saying Charles was smart, he'd have double-checked everything. I recounted that conversation to Steve as well. We both thought over the possibilities some more.

"She had to make it clear that he dropped the gun before she shot him, to cover the fact that the gun wasn't shot to pieces in his hand," Gould said.

"She took the chance that you'd still see it as murder even though he was unarmed at the moment she shot him?"

"I don't know what was going on in her head," Gould said. "And neither do you. We probably never will. In any event, according to your scenario, she covered herself there, too."

"So then she uses her one phone call to get me involved, knowing I was the only one she could call."

"And you followed your script to the letter." Gould's yellow eyes looked at me almost kindly. I was aware I was crying. He handed me a tissue.

She couldn't have known my cheap office phone would slip off the base, cross wires and register a two-hundred-dollar charge for her call to the Crystal Lake Conference Center. That was her first undoing. Only then did everything became suspect. Maybe Rhonda was sitting on a beach somewhere, fanning herself with her new millions. My face burned hotter than any sunburn.

"What are you going to do about it?" I challenged him.

"Not a damn thing."

"Huh?"

"What proof do I have?" he demanded. "All of this sounds good, but we don't have anything solid. Just a few suppositions and wild guesses. We can't prove a thing."

I was incredulous. "You mean she got away with it?"

"Got away with what? Prove what she did."

"You've got to put out an APB on her and find her!"

"That's the cops' job. I'd have to press a first-degree murder charge against her to get the cops on her trail, and I don't have a single shred of evidence that anything like this scenario ever happened."

"The phone call . . ." I cried.

"So she called her husband from your bar. Maybe she was confirming he'd arrived at the conference center. We've got no proof she actually told him to come to the cabin."

I left in a hot flush. He was another asshole.

I went home to Anne and told her of the possible drama Rhonda could have acted out, concocted by Gould and me with the fresh evidence I'd brought back from Pennsylvania. Her face kept starting to turn to a smirk, an "I told you so," but the details of the set-up kept bringing her back to the horror.

"She's a monster," Anne breathed. "And she sucked you right in."

"We can't prove a thing, remember? Gould isn't going to do anything without proof. And maybe this all is an illusion. Maybe it really happened the way we first thought."

"What do you think?" Anne quizzed me.

"I told you, I don't *know!*" I screamed at her and ran into my room. Radar licked the tears as I cried.

I lay awake and wished that I had never gotten "bored" with Anne but instead had used all that excess energy to recreate romance, to go to counseling again, to do something. But it was definitely too late.

Looking back, our problems seemed so small compared to what I had just been through. I didn't know if Anne was lying in her bed wide awake the way I was or not. I just knew I needed to talk to somebody. Really, I needed to be hugged. But it wouldn't be fair to ask for that.

At some point I decided I had to risk it. If I went into her room, all she could do would be to kick me out again.

I stood outside the door, trembling. I remembered the last time I'd stood in this doorway, prepared to tell her I was going to start seeing other women. Getting up that courage was the hardest thing I'd ever done in my life. Asking for her forgiveness was going to be even harder.

"Anne," I started.

"I'm awake. Come on in." She made no move to get out of bed. The Pom growled at me. Anne tapped his foxy snout and he burrowed under the sheet, pouting.

"Anne . . ." I couldn't go on.

"You want my forgiveness . . ."

I nodded.

". . . and you want us to get back together like nothing ever happened." Her voice was cold.

I paused to think, and chose my words carefully. "I'm sorry, I wasn't asking that. I just wanted to talk. But I wish you could forgive me. This is a mistake, it's too soon." I turned to leave.

"So you're not asking to get back together." Those blue eyes pierced through me.

I shook my head no. A tear dripped off my chin.

She sighed. "I'm sorry, too." She maneuvered herself out of the waterbed and stood beside me, an awkward arm over my shoulder. We cried in each other's arms.

"I'm glad you didn't come begging, asking me to take you back," she finally said, putting me a solid step away from her so that we could look at each other. "I often wondered, the past months, what I would say if you did. And I'd decided I could never take you back."

She picked up the Shih Tzu and ruffled her shaggy fur. "These last months have been terrible for me. I know I haven't shown it, but that's the kind of person I am. I never dreamed that you would leave me. I thought we were set for life."

The Shih Tzu licked her face. "I never took you seriously when you said that you felt like I was always in control. Controlling you. I know we didn't have sex much anymore, but that was okay with me. I felt comfortable with you, knowing it was there when we both wanted it. I didn't need sex, and I didn't think you did, either. Obviously, we didn't talk about it."

I nodded, listening.

"You fell for someone else instead, a manipulative little tramp. You deserved each other. And then she turns out to be some kind of demon."

"I didn't *know* she was like that! How could I?"

My interruption made no difference to Anne. She continued, "I'm sorry that it didn't work out for you, I truly am. I'm very glad she didn't kill you the way she apparently killed Lydia and Karen, and her husband. But I can't believe how stupid you were through this all."

Her words stung, but I decided to continue to listen rather than attempt to defend myself anymore. I owed her that.

"Maybe it's midlife crisis, I don't know. You fell in lust and lost your brains. Maybe you'll regain your senses again, but I don't think it will matter. I won't be able to put all that information aside as if it never happened. I trusted you, Laney, and now I can't trust you again. It really is over." The look in her eyes demanded that I see it her way. "I loved you so much, and I should have had us separate right away. This is too hard. Maybe you'd better move out."

I slumped against the wall. She was right. Living together any longer was going to be too hard. It really was over. "I wanted us to still be friends —"

"We are," she interrupted me.

"No, not the way we once were, not after all we've been through. Maybe someday. I'll find a place to live as soon as possible."

Radar was waiting to comfort me back in my — Rob's — room.

Her attorney and tax consultant had the papers ready in a few days. She gave me the bar in exchange for my share in the house. I agreed it was fair. I finally made Carmen manager and turned almost all of the operations over to her.

I told Kitt Meyers, the women's music mogul for whom I'd been doing some PR, that I was looking for a place to stay. She lives in a big house in Sherman Oaks south of Ventura Boulevard and needed someone to move into the carriage house. So now I'm part caretaker, part business manager, mainly when she's out of town, and in return I get free rent and too big of a salary.

As long as I keep Radar out of the pool, she has the run of the place, since Kitt has three acres totally fenced in. Radar's services are needed as well, as live-in guard dog. The carriage house is as big as the house in Silverlake. I'm settling in.

But the bar's always there. Why give up a business that stays in the black? I'm going to hold out against the strip malls as long as I can.

Kitt's a real flirt — nothing you can take seriously, but she's helping my self-esteem. No, I'm not going to sleep with her. I may have finally learned a little something about life. That big five-O is looming, so it's about time.

I called Max and spent an evening down at the bar, telling her all that happened. I seemed to need to talk about what had happened so that I could believe it myself and come to terms with it — the same advice I'd given Rhonda the last time I saw her. Max was more sympathetic than I expected, guffawing at all the right times, patting my shoulder at the other right times. "I'm not going to say I told you so," she made it a point to say, dropping ashes onto my Reeboks.

"I look back at the past year and I'm ashamed," I told her. "Every word Anne said when she kicked me out was true. Now I have to rebuild my life."

"Don't beat yourself," Max said, blowing smoke too close to my face. I coughed discreetly. She apologized and aimed her smoke rings the other direction.

"It's as if I'm just out of high school again and deciding all over what to do with myself," I mused aloud. "Maybe I hid behind Anne all those years and never grew up."

"Yeah, but some of it's Anne's fault, too," Max reassured me. "You two weren't the first lesbian couple to slide into mother-daughter roles. You know, when you started to talk about changing your butch-femme roles, I used to think Anne was the real butch." She snickered.

"*What?*" I grabbed Max by the chin. "You never told me that."

"Hell no, you think I'm crazy? Get your hands off me, you old coot."

We wrestled in mock anger. She managed to spill her cold beer down my shirt and I shook my Diet Pepsi can and doused her good. That's what friends are for.

I thought about it more later. When I quit drinking I turned my need for something to make my life pain-free and safe over to Anne, who was only too happy to comply.

But waiting underneath was that compulsion to find someone exciting, take a chance, make a mess of things — all ready to jump out when Rhonda waved her finger. Max said it right, the hardest part was to get beyond beating on myself.

My AA sponsor is starting to talk to me as if I'm an adult, not a dumb shit teetering on the edge. At meetings people take me for granted again; they've focused on the next drunk trying to get it together. I guess that's another sign I'm back on firm ground. Maybe for the first time.

I was starting to put the Rhonda business behind me when I got another call from Gould. "There's a squad car on its way to get you," he said, sending a chill down my spine. He verified my Sherman Oaks address. "We've found something we need you to take a look at."

"What?" My mind was reeling. All the old emotions tumbled around inside like in a clothes dryer.

"The police found a body and you may be able to identify it."

"What . . ."

"I'll tell you the whole story when you get here."

The squad car took me to an alley off Glendale Boulevard in Echo Park, in a hilly area of abandoned warehouses, old movie lots, and illegal sweatshops making cheap clothes. I recognized the name of the dead-end street as one where the Hillside Strangler had dumped a young prostitute's body in the late seventies.

The nearest house nestled in a dip in the hill, its garage on the other side of the dip, accessible from the alley via two dirt ruts almost invisible through the weeds. A badly cracked, paved parking lot for a boarded-up factory was on the other side of the alley. Graffiti on the factory proclaimed the territory as belonging to the 18th Street gang, though the Diamonds were contenders.

Three police cars, lights flashing, and a half-dozen city, county and state cars parked in the weeds around the garage. The hook on the rear of a tow truck held the steel garage door partially open, with jacks propped in the three-foot crawl space.

Uniformed police and men in suits got on their knees and rolled inside the dark garage, using an old Army blanket to protect their clothes. A woman in a white lab coat applied cream from a jar to everyone's upper lip and handed flashlights to those heading inside.

"Laney, over here," Gould shouted. When I opened the squad car door I gagged. Liquified toast and coffee hit the weeds in front of me and splashed on my Reeboks. The woman ran over and smeared the minty jelly on my lip, making it tingle and deadening my sense of smell.

"We think we found Rhonda," Gould told me when he reached me. He brushed dirt off his navy flannel knees and rear and grabbed me by the arm. "You're going to have to go in there. You're the only one at this stage who can say for sure. Her family can't get here for days."

"What . . ." I let myself be pulled toward the garage.

"Apparently she came back here to check on the car — maybe to get rid of fingerprints — and the metal spring on the door snapped. When that baby slammed shut, there was no way out. Watch your head." He motioned toward the propped door. "It's pretty bad in there. Brace yourself." He slipped under the door first. I did not want to go but I followed.

His flashlight showed a hulking black Chevy that took up all but a few feet on either side of the one-car garage. Spider webs hung from the corners of the windowless cement-block shell. I couldn't smell anything but mint, but I imagined what the inside of a dark, cold garage would normally smell like: oil drips and sweet antifreeze and gasoline and mold. I thought I saw the tip of a hairless tail disappear under the car.

The back door to the Chevy was open; we had to close it to get past and look inside. A wriggling body of slime curled in fetal position in the back seat. The wriggling came from thousands of white maggots.

At first glance a dry head seemed to be on the floor, but the mound of short, straight black hair was a wig. Red-gold curls hung limp over the side of the cracked plastic seatcover, soggy from the slime. I could see teeth, and bone, what may have been eye sockets. Sunk into the ooze were the like-new jeans and the red plaid shirt that I had seen many times before.

A denim satchel lay on the front seat, its contents removed, next to an empty bottle of rubbing alcohol, clean white cloths, and a crumpled bus transfer. Flies dive-bombed the corpse and us.

"Can you tell if it's her?" Gould's whisper seemed appropriate.

"Those are her clothes and purse. I can't tell anything else. What happened to her purse?"

"The detectives have the contents outside. Her fingerprints were on it, her ID was intact, but we can't go on that, or even on her clothes, in case there was foul play. We'll have to call in some other specialists and get her dental records from her parents. At least you could ID her clothes."

I couldn't look anymore. I stood up, gagged again and looked around the garage for some relief from the scene inside the car. Soiled tissues indicated that Rhonda had designated one corner of the garage as her bathroom. She'd tried to climb on top of the car to hammer at the roof, which showed some dents but which had held. Whoever built this garage was defending it against any kind of break-in, and thus against a breakout as well.

"She used the car's jack to try to get out, but it couldn't get a grip on that steel door or on anything else." Gould swung the flashlight around the interior. "She apparently tried to drive out, but the battery's dead. Probably was dead already when she tried. Old car. The kind the public thinks gang members drive."

Arcing his flashlight beam, he showed me the snapped steel spring. "Let's get out of here," Gould said. We scrambled back under the door. We kept on going until we were well into the middle of the decrepit parking lot. I let my shallow, quick breaths return to normal. The mint cream was not quite strong enough.

"How did you find her?" I asked.

"The guy who owns the garage called us. He said

he rented it to a young woman with short black hair who paid for it a year in advance. Cash, natch. When the year was up, he went down to see about renting it again and couldn't get the door up. So he called the tow truck to pry it open. When they got it cracked, the smell overpowered him, and he called the police. And here we are. You're sure it's her clothes."

"I'm sure. The clothes, the hair —"

"I figured as much. She'd wanted a garage where nobody would see her, and she got it. Oh, by the way, she never got the big money. I made some calls after you told me about your trip to her hometown. The insurance company issued a draft right away — guess that's standard practice — but when she took it to her bank to cash it, they said there'd be a six-week hold while they verified her signature, or some such story. Banks do that on very large checks. She never picked up the money, so police figure she got trapped before the six weeks were up."

I nodded, still fighting down what was left of breakfast.

"She didn't spend that much from what she got selling the cars and furniture. The Rasmussen family was scouring that prenuptial agreement with a fine-tooth comb looking for loopholes, so they got everything else tied up pretty fast. It must have galled her while she was waiting to die. All that money just sitting there, and for what?"

I tried to absorb all this information. My stomach kept churning. "How long do you think she's been there?" I asked.

"We're bringing in a forensic entomologist to figure it out."

"A what?"

"Bug specialist. They'll check out how many cycles of flies lived in the body to determine how far along the decomposition is — sorry, you asked."

"I think I saw a rat, too . . ." I left that question unasked, but he answered it anyway.

"Rats don't eat anything that's turned. Probably at the start . . ." Trying to control my breathing, I thought about what Rhonda's last days must have been like.

"Remember when you told me you'd gone to Rhonda's house and told her that she needed to talk, to figure out with you exactly what Charles had done, and you mentioned the Chevy? What exactly did she say?"

"Umm." I tried to recall. "Something like, 'Charles is smart, he'd double-check everything.' "

"So she came back to double-check everything. Probably because you'd made her wonder if she'd left a print, though she had to have cleaned the car off before that."

"Don't blame this on me." Repulsed, I glared at him.

"I didn't mean it that way. What I meant is that you can take credit for the fact that Rhonda didn't get away with the perfect crime. Kinda makes up for being her stooge, helping her set it up."

Somehow it didn't make me feel any better. Despite what she'd done, I felt mainly sorrow for Rhonda. I would always miss the Rhonda I'd thought she'd been. And I'd never be able to forget this proof of who she really was.

I took in the scene one last time, knowing I would have nightmares the rest of my life. I could have loved her, the Rhonda she'd shown me. My anger was gone at the other Rhonda. She'd paid the ultimate price. So had I.

An "Action News" van with a television satellite on the roof turned into the parking lot.

Gould and I walked toward the officers who were waiting with the paperwork.

A few of the publications of

THE NAIAD PRESS, INC.
P.O. Box 10543 • Tallahassee, Florida 32302
Phone (904) 539-5965

Mail orders welcome. Please include 15% postage.

SILVERLAKE HEAT: A Novel of Suspense by Carol Schmidt. 240 pp. Rhonda is as hot as Laney's dreams.	ISBN 1-56280-031-0	$9.95
LOVE, ZENA BETH by Diane Salvatore. 224 pp. The most talked about lesbian novel of the nineties!	ISBN 1-56280-030-2	9.95
A DOORYARD FULL OF FLOWERS by Isabel Miller. 160 pp. Stories incl. 2 sequels to *Patience and Sarah.*	ISBN 1-56280-029-9	9.95
MURDER BY TRADITION by Katherine V. Forrest. 288 pp. A Kate Delafield Mystery. 4th in a series.	ISBN 1-56280-002-7	9.95
THE EROTIC NAIAD edited by Katherine V. Forrest & Barbara Grier. 224 pp. Love stories by Naiad Press authors.	ISBN 1-56280-026-4	12.95
DEAD CERTAIN by Claire McNab. 224 pp. 5th Det. Insp. Carol Ashton mystery.	ISBN 1-56280-027-2	9.95
CRAZY FOR LOVING by Jaye Maiman. 320 pp. 2nd Robin Miller mystery.	ISBN 1-56280-025-6	9.95
STONEHURST by Barbara Johnson. 176 pp. Passionate regency romance.	ISBN 1-56280-024-8	9.95
INTRODUCING AMANDA VALENTINE by Rose Beecham. 256 pp. An Amanda Valentine Mystery — 1st in a series.	ISBN 1-56280-021-3	9.95
UNCERTAIN COMPANIONS by Robbi Sommers. 204 pp. Steamy, erotic novel.	ISBN 1-56280-017-5	9.95
A TIGER'S HEART by Lauren W. Douglas. 240 pp. Fourth Caitlin Reece Mystery.	ISBN 1-56280-018-3	9.95
PAPERBACK ROMANCE by Karin Kallmaker. 256 pp. A delicious romance.	ISBN 1-56280-019-1	9.95
MORTON RIVER VALLEY by Lee Lynch. 304 pp. Lee Lynch at her best!	ISBN 1-56280-016-7	9.95
THE LAVENDER HOUSE MURDER by Nikki Baker. 224 pp. A Virginia Kelly Mystery. Second in a series.	ISBN 1-56280-012-4	9.95
PASSION BAY by Jennifer Fulton. 224 pp. Passionate romance, virgin beaches, tropical skies.	ISBN 1-56280-028-0	9.95
STICKS AND STONES by Jackie Calhoun. 208 pp. Contemporary lesbian lives and loves.	ISBN 1-56280-020-5	9.95

DELIA IRONFOOT by Jeane Harris. 192 pp. Adventure for Delia and Beth in the Utah mountains. ISBN 1-56280-014-0 9.95

UNDER THE SOUTHERN CROSS by Claire McNab. 192 pp. Romantic nights Down Under. ISBN 1-56280-011-6 9.95

RIVERFINGER WOMEN by Elana Nachman/Dykewomon. 208 pp. Classic Lesbian/feminist novel. ISBN 1-56280-013-2 8.95

A CERTAIN DISCONTENT by Cleve Boutell. 240 pp. A unique coterie of women. ISBN 1-56280-009-4 9.95

GRASSY FLATS by Penny Hayes. 256 pp. Lesbian romance in the '30s. ISBN 1-56280-010-8 9.95

A SINGULAR SPY by Amanda K. Williams. 192 pp. 3rd spy novel featuring Lesbian agent Madison McGuire. ISBN 1-56280-008-6 8.95

THE END OF APRIL by Penny Sumner. 240 pp. A Victoria Cross Mystery. First in a series. ISBN 1-56280-007-8 8.95

A FLIGHT OF ANGELS by Sarah Aldridge. 240 pp. Romance set at the National Gallery of Art ISBN 1-56280-001-9 9.95

HOUSTON TOWN by Deborah Powell. 208 pp. A Hollis Carpenter mystery. Second in a series. ISBN 1-56280-006-X 8.95

KISS AND TELL by Robbi Sommers. 192 pp. Scorching stories by the author of *Pleasures.* ISBN 1-56280-005-1 9.95

STILL WATERS by Pat Welch. 208 pp. Second in the Helen Black mystery series. ISBN 0-941483-97-5 9.95

MURDER IS GERMANE by Karen Saum. 224 pp. The 2nd Brigid Donovan mystery. ISBN 0-941483-98-3 8.95

TO LOVE AGAIN by Evelyn Kennedy. 208 pp. Wildly romantic love story. ISBN 0-941483-85-1 9.95

IN THE GAME by Nikki Baker. 192 pp. A Virginia Kelly mystery. First in a series. ISBN 01-56280-004-3 9.95

AVALON by Mary Jane Jones. 256 pp. A Lesbian Arthurian romance. ISBN 0-941483-96-7 9.95

STRANDED by Camarin Grae. 320 pp. Entertaining, riveting adventure. ISBN 0-941483-99-1 9.95

THE DAUGHTERS OF ARTEMIS by Lauren Wright Douglas. 240 pp. Third Caitlin Reece mystery. ISBN 0-941483-95-9 9.95

CLEARWATER by Catherine Ennis. 176 pp. Romantic secrets of a small Louisiana town. ISBN 0-941483-65-7 8.95

THE HALLELUJAH MURDERS by Dorothy Tell. 176 pp. Second Poppy Dillworth mystery. ISBN 0-941483-88-6 8.95

ZETA BASE by Judith Alguire. 208 pp. Lesbian triangle on a future Earth. ISBN 0-941483-94-0 9.95

SECOND CHANCE by Jackie Calhoun. 256 pp. Contemporary Lesbian lives and loves. ISBN 0-941483-93-2 9.95

BENEDICTION by Diane Salvatore. 272 pp. Striking,
contemporary romantic novel. ISBN 0-941483-90-8 9.95

CALLING RAIN by Karen Marie Christa Minns. 240 pp.
Spellbinding, erotic love story ISBN 0-941483-87-8 9.95

BLACK IRIS by Jeane Harris. 192 pp. Caroline's hidden past . . .
ISBN 0-941483-68-1 8.95

TOUCHWOOD by Karin Kallmaker. 240 pp. Loving, May/
December romance. ISBN 0-941483-76-2 9.95

BAYOU CITY SECRETS by Deborah Powell. 224 pp. A Hollis
Carpenter mystery. First in a series. ISBN 0-941483-91-6 9.95

COP OUT by Claire McNab. 208 pp. 4th Det. Insp. Carol Ashton
mystery. ISBN 0-941483-84-3 9.95

LODESTAR by Phyllis Horn. 224 pp. Romantic, fast-moving
adventure. ISBN 0-941483-83-5 8.95

THE BEVERLY MALIBU by Katherine V. Forrest. 288 pp. A
Kate Delafield Mystery. 3rd in a series. ISBN 0-941483-48-7 9.95

THAT OLD STUDEBAKER by Lee Lynch. 272 pp. Andy's affair
with Regina and her attachment to her beloved car.
ISBN 0-941483-82-7 9.95

PASSION'S LEGACY by Lori Paige. 224 pp. Sarah is swept into
the arms of Augusta Pym in this delightful historical romance.
ISBN 0-941483-81-9 8.95

THE PROVIDENCE FILE by Amanda Kyle Williams. 256 pp.
Second espionage thriller featuring lesbian agent Madison McGuire
ISBN 0-941483-92-4 8.95

I LEFT MY HEART by Jaye Maiman. 320 pp. A Robin Miller
Mystery. First in a series. ISBN 0-941483-72-X 9.95

THE PRICE OF SALT by Patricia Highsmith (writing as Claire
Morgan). 288 pp. Classic lesbian novel, first issued in 1952 . . .
acknowledged by its author under her own, very famous, name.
ISBN 1-56280-003-5 9.95

SIDE BY SIDE by Isabel Miller. 256 pp. From beloved author of
Patience and Sarah. ISBN 0-941483-77-0 9.95

SOUTHBOUND by Sheila Ortiz Taylor. 240 pp. Hilarious sequel
to *Faultline.* ISBN 0-941483-78-9 8.95

STAYING POWER: LONG TERM LESBIAN COUPLES
by Susan E. Johnson. 352 pp. Joys of coupledom.
ISBN 0-941-483-75-4 12.95

SLICK by Camarin Grae. 304 pp. Exotic, erotic adventure.
ISBN 0-941483-74-6 9.95

NINTH LIFE by Lauren Wright Douglas. 256 pp. A Caitlin
Reece mystery. 2nd in a series. ISBN 0-941483-50-9 8.95

PLAYERS by Robbi Sommers. 192 pp. Sizzling, erotic novel. ISBN 0-941483-73-8 9.95

MURDER AT RED ROOK RANCH by Dorothy Tell. 224 pp. First Poppy Dillworth adventure. ISBN 0-941483-80-0 8.95

LESBIAN SURVIVAL MANUAL by Rhonda Dicksion. 112 pp. Cartoons! ISBN 0-941483-71-1 8.95

A ROOM FULL OF WOMEN by Elisabeth Nonas. 256 pp. Contemporary Lesbian lives. ISBN 0-941483-69-X 9.95

MURDER IS RELATIVE by Karen Saum. 256 pp. The first Brigid Donovan mystery. ISBN 0-941483-70-3 8.95

PRIORITIES by Lynda Lyons 288 pp. Science fiction with a twist. ISBN 0-941483-66-5 8.95

THEME FOR DIVERSE INSTRUMENTS by Jane Rule. 208 pp. Powerful romantic lesbian stories. ISBN 0-941483-63-0 8.95

LESBIAN QUERIES by Hertz & Ertman. 112 pp. The questions you were too embarrassed to ask. ISBN 0-941483-67-3 8.95

CLUB 12 by Amanda Kyle Williams. 288 pp. Espionage thriller featuring a lesbian agent! ISBN 0-941483-64-9 8.95

DEATH DOWN UNDER by Claire McNab. 240 pp. 3rd Det. Insp. Carol Ashton mystery. ISBN 0-941483-39-8 9.95

MONTANA FEATHERS by Penny Hayes. 256 pp. Vivian and Elizabeth find love in frontier Montana. ISBN 0-941483-61-4 8.95

CHESAPEAKE PROJECT by Phyllis Horn. 304 pp. Jessie & Meredith in perilous adventure. ISBN 0-941483-58-4 8.95

LIFESTYLES by Jackie Calhoun. 224 pp. Contemporary Lesbian lives and loves. ISBN 0-941483-57-6 9.95

VIRAGO by Karen Marie Christa Minns. 208 pp. Darsen has chosen Ginny. ISBN 0-941483-56-8 8.95

WILDERNESS TREK by Dorothy Tell. 192 pp. Six women on vacation learning "new" skills. ISBN 0-941483-60-6 8.95

MURDER BY THE BOOK by Pat Welch. 256 pp. A Helen Black Mystery. First in a series. ISBN 0-941483-59-2 9.95

BERRIGAN by Vicki P. McConnell. 176 pp. Youthful Lesbian — romantic, idealistic Berrigan. ISBN 0-941483-55-X 8.95

LESBIANS IN GERMANY by Lillian Faderman & B. Eriksson. 128 pp. Fiction, poetry, essays. ISBN 0-941483-62-2 8.95

THERE'S SOMETHING I'VE BEEN MEANING TO TELL YOU Ed. by Loralee MacPike. 288 pp. Gay men and lesbians coming out to their children. ISBN 0-941483-44-4 9.95

LIFTING BELLY by Gertrude Stein. Ed. by Rebecca Mark. 104 pp. Erotic poetry. ISBN 0-941483-51-7 8.95

ROSE PENSKI by Roz Perry. 192 pp. Adult lovers in a long-term relationship.	ISBN 0-941483-37-1	8.95
AFTER THE FIRE by Jane Rule. 256 pp. Warm, human novel by this incomparable author.	ISBN 0-941483-45-2	8.95
SUE SLATE, PRIVATE EYE by Lee Lynch. 176 pp. The gay folk of Peacock Alley are *all cats*.	ISBN 0-941483-52-5	8.95
CHRIS by Randy Salem. 224 pp. Golden oldie. Handsome Chris and her adventures.	ISBN 0-941483-42-8	8.95
THREE WOMEN by March Hastings. 232 pp. Golden oldie. A triangle among wealthy sophisticates.	ISBN 0-941483-43-6	8.95
RICE AND BEANS by Valeria Taylor. 232 pp. Love and romance on poverty row.	ISBN 0-941483-41-X	8.95
PLEASURES by Robbi Sommers. 204 pp. Unprecedented eroticism.	ISBN 0-941483-49-5	8.95
EDGEWISE by Camarin Grae. 372 pp. Spellbinding adventure.	ISBN 0-941483-19-3	9.95
FATAL REUNION by Claire McNab. 224 pp. 2nd Det. Inspec. Carol Ashton mystery.	ISBN 0-941483-40-1	8.95
KEEP TO ME STRANGER by Sarah Aldridge. 372 pp. Romance set in a department store dynasty.	ISBN 0-941483-38-X	9.95
HEARTSCAPE by Sue Gambill. 204 pp. American lesbian in Portugal.	ISBN 0-941483-33-9	8.95
IN THE BLOOD by Lauren Wright Douglas. 252 pp. Lesbian science fiction adventure fantasy	ISBN 0-941483-22-3	8.95
THE BEE'S KISS by Shirley Verel. 216 pp. Delicate, delicious romance.	ISBN 0-941483-36-3	8.95
RAGING MOTHER MOUNTAIN by Pat Emmerson. 264 pp. Furosa Firechild's adventures in Wonderland.	ISBN 0-941483-35-5	8.95
IN EVERY PORT by Karin Kallmaker. 228 pp. Jessica's sexy, adventuresome travels.	ISBN 0-941483-37-7	9.95
OF LOVE AND GLORY by Evelyn Kennedy. 192 pp. Exciting WWII romance.	ISBN 0-941483-32-0	8.95
CLICKING STONES by Nancy Tyler Glenn. 288 pp. Love transcending time.	ISBN 0-941483-31-2	9.95
SURVIVING SISTERS by Gail Pass. 252 pp. Powerful love story.	ISBN 0-941483-16-9	8.95
SOUTH OF THE LINE by Catherine Ennis. 216 pp. Civil War adventure.	ISBN 0-941483-29-0	8.95
WOMAN PLUS WOMAN by Dolores Klaich. 300 pp. Supurb Lesbian overview.	ISBN 0-941483-28-2	9.95
SLOW DANCING AT MISS POLLY'S by Sheila Ortiz Taylor. 96 pp. Lesbian Poetry	ISBN 0-941483-30-4	7.95

DOUBLE DAUGHTER by Vicki P. McConnell. 216 pp. A Nyla Wade Mystery, third in the series. ISBN 0-941483-26-6 8.95

HEAVY GILT by Delores Klaich. 192 pp. Lesbian detective/disappearing homophobes/upper class gay society. ISBN 0-941483-25-8 8.95

THE FINER GRAIN by Denise Ohio. 216 pp. Brilliant young college lesbian novel. ISBN 0-941483-11-8 8.95

THE AMAZON TRAIL by Lee Lynch. 216 pp. Life, travel & lore of famous lesbian author. ISBN 0-941483-27-4 8.95

HIGH CONTRAST by Jessie Lattimore. 264 pp. Women of the Crystal Palace. ISBN 0-941483-17-7 8.95

OCTOBER OBSESSION by Meredith More. Josie's rich, secret Lesbian life. ISBN 0-941483-18-5 8.95

LESBIAN CROSSROADS by Ruth Baetz. 276 pp. Contemporary Lesbian lives. ISBN 0-941483-21-5 9.95

BEFORE STONEWALL: THE MAKING OF A GAY AND LESBIAN COMMUNITY by Andrea Weiss & Greta Schiller. 96 pp., 25 illus. ISBN 0-941483-20-7 7.95

WE WALK THE BACK OF THE TIGER by Patricia A. Murphy. 192 pp. Romantic Lesbian novel/beginning women's movement. ISBN 0-941483-13-4 8.95

SUNDAY'S CHILD by Joyce Bright. 216 pp. Lesbian athletics, at last the novel about sports. ISBN 0-941483-12-6 8.95

OSTEN'S BAY by Zenobia N. Vole. 204 pp. Sizzling adventure romance set on Bonaire. ISBN 0-941483-15-0 8.95

LESSONS IN MURDER by Claire McNab. 216 pp. 1st Det. Inspec. Carol Ashton mystery — erotic tension!. ISBN 0-941483-14-2 8.95

YELLOWTHROAT by Penny Hayes. 240 pp. Margarita, bandit, kidnaps Julia. ISBN 0-941483-10-X 8.95

SAPPHISTRY: THE BOOK OF LESBIAN SEXUALITY by Pat Califia. 3d edition, revised. 208 pp. ISBN 0-941483-24-X 8.95

CHERISHED LOVE by Evelyn Kennedy. 192 pp. Erotic Lesbian love story. ISBN 0-941483-08-8 9.95

LAST SEPTEMBER by Helen R. Hull. 208 pp. Six stories & a glorious novella. ISBN 0-941483-09-6 8.95

These are just a few of the many Naiad Press titles — we are the oldest and largest lesbian/feminist publishing company in the world. Please request a complete catalog. We offer personal service; we encourage and welcome direct mail orders from individuals who have limited access to bookstores carrying our publications.